FOREST OF FIRE

RUSSELL JAMES

SEVERED PRESS

HOBART TASMANIA

FOREST OF FIRE

Dedication

For Christy,
who makes life a wonderful adventure.

Other books by Russell James

<u>Grant Coleman Adventures</u>
Cavern of the Damned
Monsters in the Clouds
Curse of the Viper King

<u>Ranger Kathy West National Park Adventures</u>
Claws

CHAPTER ONE

Professor Grant Coleman looked out at the lecture hall. Most of the seats were empty, even though his class on the Triassic Era had almost a hundred students. He could not fault the missing. It was Friday afternoon before Robeson University's Thanksgiving break. He loved to teach and even he wouldn't have been here if he wasn't required. A perfect, crisp fall day was going to waste on the other side of the windows.

"So at about 199 million years ago," Grant said, pointing a red laser at a map on the screen behind him, "tectonic forces finally won out, and began to split the supercontinent Pangea into Laurasia in the north and Gondwana in the south."

He checked the clock on the podium.

"And that's a good stopping point for today. If you don't mind getting cheated on your tuition money, I'll call this class done fifteen minutes early."

Books slammed, chairs scraped, phones dinged. The lecture hall emptied in seconds. Fire drills took longer. Grant pushed his glasses back up the bridge of his nose and gathered his notes.

A man in a business suit approached down the main aisle. He carried a thin messenger bag. He had a sharp haircut and a bright blue tie. He stopped in front of the podium.

"Professor Coleman? I'm Matt Calloway."

He held out his hand. Grant didn't shake it.

"If you are a new lawyer representing my ex-wife," Grant said, "I'm all paid up."

Calloway smiled. "No, I'm afraid I have to admit I'm a lawyer, but I'm not representing your ex-wife. I'm representing the estate of Professor Maxwell Carson."

Grant caught his breath. He gave the man's hand a slow shake. "Professor Carson died?"

"That's what brings me here. You studied under him throughout your doctoral classes?"

"Yes, he was inspirational. I literally owe my career choice to him."

"This summer, he was doing field research in China."

"At his age? He has to be 70."

"71. Well, he went missing. No contact. The Chinese government says they couldn't find a trace of him."

"How big an expedition?"

"Just himself. He'd been part of an earlier expedition, but after that ended, he returned on his own, then vanished in the Gobi Desert. Now the Chinese government has certified him as missing and dead, but his wife won't accept it. She wants to send a party in to find him. One that will stay under the Chinese radar. She wants someone who knows paleontology and knows Professor Carson. That person will know where to look for him. She thinks that person is you."

"I would love to help, really, but I can't leave in the middle of the semester."

"Arrangements have all been made. Private jets, expert guides. You'll be back before your afternoon class the Monday after Thanksgiving break."

Grant didn't have anything planned for the Thanksgiving break. And he owed Professor Carson more than he could ever repay.

"I can do that," Grant said.

"Excellent."

The lawyer reached into his bag and pulled out a sealed legal sized envelope with Grant's name handwritten on the outside. Grant recognized Professor Carson's writing immediately. He'd seen enough of it scribbled over every research paper he'd written.

"The professor left this for you," the lawyer said, "in the event anything went wrong during his expedition."

"For me? What's in it?"

"No idea. I was legally bound to deliver it unopened. A car will be by your house to pick you up at 5:00 PM."

The lawyer shook Grant's hand and then closed his bag and headed for the door.

"There have been so many new discoveries coming out of China," Grant called after him. "Any idea what he was searching for?"

"I'm no scientist," the lawyer said over his shoulder. "And he must have been using a nickname for whatever it was. He kept telling his wife he was looking for dragons."

CHAPTER TWO

Twenty years ago. Professor Maxwell Carson's paleontology lab.

A wet cloth smacked Grant Coleman in the face. He looked up from the fossil he was freeing from a block of sandstone. Fellow grad student Mike Rabon grinned from ear to ear at the other end of the great slab.

For two years, the duo had been lab partners and partners in crime, though the crime portion generally came from the Rabon half of the team. The kid with the long sandy hair was always up to something, cutting some corner, taking some unnecessary risk, and usually when Grant was able to share the blame.

Outside of the bright lights over the specimen, the rest of the basement paleontology lab struggled by with dim lighting. Past finds encased in plaster sat on shelves awaiting detailed cleaning and examination. Professor Carson had recovered this particular fossil on last year's summer expedition and he'd tasked the two of them to prepare it for study.

The rag fell from Grant's face. He caught it before it hit the half-exposed skull beneath him.

"Hilarious," he said. He wadded up the rag and tossed it back. Baseball was not Grant's strong suit. The rag flew wide of its mark. Rabon, the natural athlete, effortlessly snatched it out of the air with one hand anyway. He barely seemed to move.

"C'mon, you need a break. We need a break. We've been picking at this thing for six hours and it looks like we've gotten nowhere."

"That's how it works if you want to expose the fossil without damaging it."

"You're working on the skull. You have someone to look at. I'm digging at tiny tailbones."

"It's fitting that the smarter student is exposing the brain case. Since you're generally an ass, the creature's rear area suits you better."

"There has to be someone lower on the totem pole to do this kind of grunt work."

"We're grad students. We're so low on the totem pole, we're buried with the base of it." Grant rubbed his eyes. "It'll be great to be a professor and have my own grad students doing this stuff."

"You have to dream bigger than that," Mike said. "You want to be broke your whole life? Private enterprise is the way to go."

"Digging for hire?"

"Absolutely. Read lots of stories on it. Rich people pay rich rewards to own something as stupid as bits of fossilized poop."

"And how does private digging advance science?"

"Damn, Grant, how many dinosaurs do you think are buried on this planet? Millions. So one goes in some fat cat's trophy case. Big deal. Billionaires squirrel away priceless art, Picassos, Monets, Michealangelos. All out of the public view. Those works are one-of-a-kind and you're okay with that."

"A private collector doesn't record provenance for the fossil, doesn't make it accessible for research. And who knows if he'll take care of it properly."

"So if I sold one fossil to finance digging up seven more, you'd condemn me?"

Grant had to think about that one.

"See," Mike said. "I'm right, as usual. Don't worry, I'll remember all you little people when I'm filthy rich. Probably toss a little fossil cleaning work your way."

Professor Maxwell Carson entered the work area. Tall and thin, he had the weathered features earned over decades of outdoor excavations. Grant had been thrilled when the professor had accepted him as a student. Professor Carson had a national reputation in paleontology. A degree earned under his guidance meant something.

"Well, boys, how's the rock treating you?"

"Giving hard lessons," they both replied. This banter had become the standard greeting for every visit Carson made to the lab.

Carson took a large magnifying glass from his pocket and began to inspect the area where Mike was working, unearthing the tail. Then he stepped over to where Grant had cleared away the creature's jawbone. He moved back from the fossil.

"So, Mike," Carson said in his I'm-about-to-test-you voice. "What is it we've got here?"

Mike paused. "Therapod definitely. *Elaphrosaurus* from the looks so far."

Carson nodded. That was Carson's response that said "nice try." Mike's shoulders slumped.

"Where did I recover this piece?" Carson said.

Grant stepped away to the desk and flipped open a sand-blasted notebook. The pages were filled with dense, small writing. The professor used a field shorthand that combined Latin phrases, English, and some symbols for common archaeological terms. He turned to the page for the fossil they were preparing.

"Junggar Basin in western China," Grant said.

"So this theropod is probably…" Carson waited for an answer.

"*Limusaurus,*" Grant said.

"Superb! And that's why location notes mean everything."

"Funny," Grant said. "We were just discussing that same thing."

Mike grimaced.

"Some alumni will be looking at the lab this afternoon," Carson said. "Make sure it looks professional."

Carson left the room.

"Okay, that wasn't fair," Mike said. "He knows I can't read the gobbledy-gook he scribbles into his notes."

"Is it my fault you didn't take three years of Latin in high school?"

Mike went back to work on the tailbone with a bit of vengeance in his eyes and more effort in his scraping.

"We'll see in the end," he said. "One of the three of us is going to turn archaeology into real money, and I'm betting it'll be me."

CHAPTER THREE

Present Day. Grant's classroom.

As the lawyer left, Dean Malley entered Grant's classroom. The stooped, older man wore a dark suit with a tie adorned with the college logo. His long nose always reminded Grant far too much of a number of dinosaurs he'd unearthed at digs. He took being Dean of Sciences seriously. Quality of education, though, not so much. In Grant's experience, the good dean had always been a political player, with an overriding interest in optics and department position within the collegiate hierarchy. Given the news the lawyer had just broken to Grant, the last thing he wanted to do was waste time with Dean Malley.

"Professor Coleman," the dean said. "Glad I caught you before break began."

"A treat for us both."

The dean did not react to the sarcasm. "I wanted to remind you that we have a staff meeting on the Monday we return to discuss department participation in this year's alumni fundraiser."

Grant struggled to think of a bigger waste of his time. "Sure thing, I'll be there."

"Plans for Thanksgiving?"

A lightning bolt of fear that the dean was about to invite Grant to do Thanksgiving dinner shot up Grant's spine.

"Big plans. All booked up."

"Writing another of your little stories?"

Grant had published a series of adventure novels about a college professor encountering giant monsters around the world. Only he knew they were semi-autobiographical. The dean was far less thrilled with the series than his readers were. Grant wondered if the man ever read fiction.

"I just finished writing *Curse of the Viper King* about a giant snake in the Amazon. I'll autograph you a copy when it comes out."

"I'd much rather see some academic research, something published and peer reviewed. That's the kind of work that gets our college and your department noticed."

"The college president said he's happy that my books get us a lot of social media exposure and drive in more applications."

It really stuck in Dean Malley's craw that the president supported Grant writing novels that readers devoured, instead of dusty research papers a few other professors might read.

"Don't let scribbling on your little stories cut into your academic work. Or your commitment to our alumni fundraising."

"I wouldn't dream of it."

Dean Malley looked like he was unsure how seriously Grant was taking this wet noodle of a tongue lashing. "See you for the faculty meeting, then."

The dean left the room and Grant tore open the envelope from Professor Carson. The letter within had been handwritten on plain white paper.

Grant,

I am leaving this letter for you in case I do not return. Last year, in the final days of my department's expedition to the Gobi Desert, I found an amazing new fossil, an entirely new species. Where archaeopteryx and others are a link between dinosaurs and birds, what I found was a different evolutionary branch, a link to true flying dinosaurs, a creature unlike anything anyone has ever catalogued.

With my permit due to expire, there wasn't time to excavate the fossil. I certainly did not want to tell the Chinese what I'd found. The Chinese government is happy to have you discover something, but not at all happy to have you take your discovery home. If they knew what I'd discovered, by the time I came back, the area would have been nothing but a crater, and everything that had been inside would be gone forever.

I've arranged to return, financed this one myself. My college wasn't going to cough up since I could not very well tell them what

I'd found either. But I have a bad feeling about this. Maybe I'm just paranoid now, but… Well I'm leaving this for you. If anything happens to me, know that something amazing needs to be uncovered in China. You were my most promising student. Perhaps you will find it.

-Maxwell

Underneath were a set of cryptic symbols. Grant smiled at them. They were part of the professor's personal shorthand he'd always used in field notes. Grant was the one who always transcribed the notes, so he still remembered some of the code after all these years. He jotted down the translation and it turned out to be latitude and longitude coordinates. Grant typed them into his laptop and a search served up a map with a red dot in Inner Mongolia, a province in China. The location sat beside a seasonal lake and the runoff stream that fed it from the mountains.

Grant nodded in approval at the location. Prime dino hunting territory. Undisturbed by man, but frequently disturbed by flash floods during the monsoons. The water would scour away sand and leave all sorts of goodies exposed. Professor Carson knew his stuff.

Carson also knew enough to be prepared for such an expedition, especially having already been there. The land was unforgiving, a desert in every sense of the word. Lucky for Grant he was going with a well-financed expedition in a private jet. He could get used to that in a hurry.

He needed to get home and get packed. He only had a few hours before his 5:00 PM pickup and he didn't even know what the weather was like on that side of the world.

CHAPTER FOUR

A taxi picked up Grant and his suitcase right on time. But the driver didn't take Grant to the airport, at least not the commercial airport he expected. Instead the taxi let him out at the small municipal airport just outside of town. Private pilots flew Cessnas out there on the weekends.

"You sure this is the right place?" Grant asked.

The taxi driver held up a sheet of paper so Grant could see it from the back seat. "One fare, your house address to county airport. Prepaid including tip."

This didn't seem right. The airport did not have a passenger terminal. The closest equivalent was an airfield manager's office.

"Let's check that building and see what's going on," Grant said.

The driver stopped the taxi beside the small concrete box of an office. Grant got out, carrying his bag. He stepped over to the front door. He found it locked. Then he turned around in time to see the taxi departing.

"Well this is a great start," he said.

He walked around the office building to an apron with several small propeller-driven private planes on it. All were covered, tied down, or in some other way indicated to be unprepared for flight. The one with flat tires looked like it might never be ready again. Grant walked through the row of planes to the runway.

A few miles away to his right and a few thousand feet up, a landing light popped on. The white dot turned into a spot and then turned into an approaching plane. It touched down and taxied over to Grant.

The private jet was a solid glossy black with tail numbers in small gold lettering. Several oval windows ran down the side. The pilot cut the engines back to a mild scream and the plane rolled to a stop beside Grant. The door on the side opened and a stairway folded out and touched the ground.

A Chinese woman stepped out of the plane. She wore khaki-colored cargo pants and a blue button-down shirt. Her black hair was pulled back in a short pony tail. The look on her broad face was one of contempt.

"You are Dr. Coleman?" she shouted over the engine.

"Would there be someone else standing here with a suitcase at 5:00?"

"Get onboard. We wasting time." She headed back up the stairway.

"Great to meet you, too," Grant said.

He lugged his suitcase up the steep steps. His promises to get in better shape after his last adventure in the Amazon had, surprisingly, gone unfulfilled. However, his promise to eat multiple cheeseburgers upon his return had been flawlessly observed. He panted as he heaved his bag into the cabin.

The woman pulled the steps up and closed the door behind him. She stuck her head into the cockpit and spat a few commands in Chinese to the pilot. The engines revved and the plane began to move. She turned back to Grant.

"I am Laoxin," she said. "I am hired as your interpreter and guide on this expedition."

"We're on our way to China?"

"We were until we diverted here to get you. Now back on our way."

"Sorry to delay you."

He turned to look at the cabin. A half-dozen seats faced him. They weren't any more luxurious than ones he'd sat in on tiny commercial planes, which meant not luxurious at all. There was no stack of new camping equipment in the back of the cabin, just a few bags in a pile. Where was the well-stocked bar and the doting flight attendant?

More importantly, where was the team? All the seats were empty.

Laoxin sat down in the front seat. "Seatbelt on now," she said over her shoulder.

Grant sat down and strapped in. From the cockpit, the captain began a conversation with the FAA by radio to file an international flight plan.

The lavatory door at the rear of the cabin opened and closed. Grant looked over his shoulder and his jaw dropped. Mike Rabon stood there adjusting his belt buckle.

"Mike?"

"Grant!"

Mike sat behind him and they shook hands. Mike had put on some weight and gotten a decent haircut, but he still had that same salesman's smile that had helped him glide through a lot of college classes.

"I thought how cool it was that we were stopping to pick you up," Mike said. "How long has it been?"

"Almost twenty years." Grant didn't want to make the situation awkward dwelling on why there had been such a gap since they'd both studied under Professor Carson.

"You've made quite a name for yourself."

"Thank you." Grant's chest swelled. He was proud that Mike had apparently read some of his paleontological papers. Maybe he'd been watching Grant's career from afar, hopefully with a tinge of jealousy.

"I'm honored to share the flight with a true literary giant." The sarcasm couldn't be missed.

Grant's ego hissed as it deflated. He'd written three thriller novels based on the adventures he'd had. They'd been modest successes. One had been optioned to be made into a movie. It wasn't that he was ashamed of them. He thought they were good books. But in this scenario, he'd have been happier to be recognized as a paleontologist.

"It's no big deal," Grant said.

"Oh, no. Don't downplay your accomplishments."

Mike whipped out his phone and began tapping at the screen. The last thing Grant wanted was to start this expedition with a Google search of his collected works.

"Look," Grant said. "I don't think a cell signal will—"

"I got it!" Mike said.

"Hey, the plane has wi-fi," Grant sighed. "Thank God."

The phone displayed Grant's author page on Amazon. Grant made a grab for it. Mike held it straight up over his head, facing down.

"Well, well," Mike said. "A master of wordplay among us. *Cavern of the Damned, Monsters in the Clouds*. Giant scorpions. Dinosaurs. The Renaissance Literature Appreciation class you took sure didn't go to waste."

This kind of response was exactly why Grant tried to keep his professional career and his writing career in separate boxes.

"It's a hobby that pays royalties," Grant said. Ready to find another subject, he turned to Laoxin. "Laoxin, where is the rest of the team?"

"Meet them in China."

The jet engines spun up to a roar and obliterated the possibility of any more conversation. The plane taxied to the runway and then threw everyone back in their seats as it blasted down the asphalt.

Grant closed his eyes and wondered if he could sleep all the way to China.

CHAPTER FIVE

Sixteen hours.

That's how long the flight was supposed to last. Grant didn't think planes like this carried enough fuel to fly for that long. Or that the pilot could go that long without sleeping.

Maybe he puts the plane on autopilot and takes a nap.

Grant banished the thought. He'd rather live with the fantasy that the pilot was on top of everything every second.

The seats weren't the only thing about this flight that was coach class. There was no meal service. There were two six-packs of bottled water, a box of peanut butter sandwich crackers, and a few sleeves of Oreos. They were not going to starve to death, but that option might look better as the flight progressed.

There was also no in-flight entertainment system. He guessed he could stream movies on his phone, but Grant hated trying to read or watch anything on such a small screen. Mike had fallen asleep to pass the time, but Grant couldn't seem to manage that either.

Laoxin sat in the first row, awake and looking at a satellite map. Grant realized how little he knew about what they were doing. He got up and sat beside her. The location on her map was close to the one Grant had found using the coordinates from Carson's letter.

"So where are we landing this thing?"

She pointed to a spot on the map that looked like a few huts and a mile of superhighway connected to nothing at either end. "We land there. Abandoned Chinese airstrip. Close to Carson dig site. Short drive."

She pointed to a spot on the map by the dry lake bed marked with an X, a dozen miles from the airstrip. It wasn't quite where

Carson had pinpointed his find with the coded coordinates in his letter. The professor must have been hunting further afield when he discovered his fossil. No wonder no one else knew about his prize. Grant decided to keep that information to himself for now. Carson would be furious when they found him if he discovered that Grant had somehow made the Chinese aware of Carson's secret fossil.

"Customs will be meeting us at the airstrip?" Grant said.

"No Customs. No border agents. No government."

"Whoa! I didn't think that lawyer saying we'd be flying under Chinese radar meant literally flying under Chinese radar. I'm smuggling myself into a totalitarian dictatorship?"

"Chinese never let us in, say professor is dead. This is what Mrs. Carson pay me for. Pull strings with People's Liberation Army. Fly in. Fly out."

It was hard to believe that a passenger jet could penetrate Chinese air defense when a fighter jet couldn't, but Laoxin was betting her life that it could, and now he was betting his.

"I'll go out on a limb and guess that you are native Chinese."

"Born in Hong Kong before reunification. I enlist in the People's Liberation Army but see the future there, and for China, is very dark. Use Hong Kong birthright to leverage exit visa to United States."

"Aren't you afraid of going back?"

"I can blend in." She looked Grant up and down. "Not you."

"Thanks. Sure you didn't work for the Department of Tourism instead of the PLA?"

"Stay with me. Do what I say. Chinese jail is not good."

"I've read their Yelp reviews. I'll be right by your side."

Laoxin returned to studying the map. Grant went back to his seat. The woman kind of gave him the creeps. A little from her present-tense-only English, a little from her emotionless responses. Both of those together didn't build a sense of trust, and she'd just made it clear that he'd need to trust her implicitly to get in and out of China in one piece.

Maybe flying commercial airlines in coach wasn't so bad after all.

CHAPTER SIX

The jet's touchdown jolted Grant awake.

He slid open the window shade to reveal nothing but darkness beyond where the landing light lit the runway. Thrust reversers screamed, brakes grabbed. The change in momentum threw him forward. Grant's seatbelt cinched him under his belly and tried to sever him in two. The jet nearly stopped, then turned left and crawled to a small apron beside the runway. A large camouflage net shaded one section and the plane rolled in beneath it.

Mike stretched from his seat. "Welcome to the People's Republic," he said with a yawn. "What time is it here?"

"Half past tomorrow," Grant said.

Laoxin stood up as the plane stopped. "Get your bags. Wait on plane until I call you."

She opened the door and dropped the folding stairs. A rush of dry, cold air blew into the plane. A thin layer of grit fogged Grant's glasses and he had to wipe them clean with his shirt. The air smelled musty, with an overlay of burning wood.

He and Mike went to the back to get their bags. Mike shouldered a battered military-style sand-colored rucksack. Grant found his rollaboard suitcase and felt like a misguided tourist. A long olive drab duffel bag remained on the floor.

"Is this yours?" Grant asked.

"Yeah. We'll leave it for now."

Laoxin poked her head back in the door. "Come now. Quick."

The two shuffled to the door. Grant was first down. He teetered as he tried to balance his suitcase down the steep, short steps. At the last step, he looked up to see a large, boxy truck with a high canvas cover over the rear bed. Beyond it rose the burned-out shells of old flight hangars. In front of the truck stood two stout men who could pass as warriors for Genghis Khan. They wore heavy jackets and boxy hats against the cold. Both carried battered AK-47 rifles. Laoxin led Grant and Mike between them to the rear of the truck.

"These men are your personal protection," Laoxin said.

"Protection from…?" Grant said.

"Everyone else."

Laoxin pointed up into the bed of the truck. The two climbed in with their bags and sat on wooden benches along the sides. Laoxin took a GPS device from her pocket and looked at the display. She led the guards around to the cab. As they passed, Mike said a few words in Chinese to one of the men. The guard grunted a few words back.

"You speak Chinese?" Grant said.

"Over the years I picked up enough to get by," Mike said.

"Enough to get by with hired thugs?"

"We've been traveling in different circles, buddy."

"I've been teaching college," Grant said. "I'm afraid to ask about your different circle."

"Never ask questions you don't want the answer to."

That response didn't sit well with Grant. After graduation, Grant had gotten an academic position. Mike hadn't even applied for one. Instead he'd hired on under Angelo Destro, a man whose thin veneer of legitimate fossil sales barely concealed a deep history of black marketeering. Grant had tried to change Mike's mind. Mike's defense turned furious. The two hadn't spoken since, though Grant had heard rumors through the years of some less-than-legal excavations tied to Mike's name. It didn't seem like Mike would be about to deny them.

The truck started up with a diesel clatter and lurched forward. It rolled off the edge of the apron and into sandy dirt. The driver gunned it, accelerating to a rate Grant felt completely unwarranted for what seemed like a cross-country trip in the dark. The truck bounced over ruts and crashed against rocks. The two men were thrown around and had to hold onto the bench to stay seated.

"This is like a scene from one of your books," Mike shouted from the other side of the truck.

Grant hoped that wasn't even remotely true. His books never ended well for the people traveling in the backs of trucks like this one.

CHAPTER SEVEN

An hour later, or maybe it was a month, it felt like the latter to Grant, the truck finally came to a stop. The sun had risen and sat low over a smoggy, eastern horizon. Its weak strength didn't promise a bump in the chilly temperature any time soon.

"I guess we get out here," Mike said.

"I'm willing to if only to wake up my butt," Grant said.

The two climbed out. Laoxin was already waiting. The two guards had taken up positions a few meters to either side, looking outward, weapons at the ready.

"This is camp," she said. "Last place anyone contact Professor Carson. We start search here."

"That was months ago," Mike said.

"And I'm assuming the Chinese have been through this place with leaf blowers looking for clues," Grant added.

"We check anyway," Laoxin said. "Only place to start."

They stood where the edge of the drying lake had lapped the shore last spring. Salt crystals dappled the high-water mark. The ground sloped up gently from here. The now-dry stream that had fed the lake came off some steeper, craggy ground to the west. The current lake was just a silver shimmer to the east.

A hundred meters in front of them yawned a deep dig that ran a dozen meters long and almost as wide. The large, tan canvas that had shielded the diggers from the sun had collapsed on top of the excavation, leaving the section closest to them exposed.

Laoxin and one of the guards walked down to the dig.

"The professor would be furious that the tarp hadn't been better secured and had contaminated the dig site," Grant said.

"He was a stickler," Mike said.

Grant and Mike followed Laoxin.

They got to the edge of the dig. A set of steps descended into the pit and under the corner of the collapsed canvas. The guard took up a watchful stance beside them. Laoxin snapped back the edge of the canvas and dropped down into the pit.

Grant followed. The dig had multiple levels, with each labeled section divided by strings on sticks. A rack of sifting screens sat at the far end. Three stubby shovels lay in a stack. Blown sand covered everything.

Mike climbed down and went to one of the excavation sections. He picked up a whisk brush from a shelf and swept away the loose sand. Laoxin walked down to the excavation's far end.

"No one was working here when the place was abandoned," Grant said.

"This look like work site," Laoxin said.

"It was," Grant said. "But if a calamity struck while Carson was working here, the sifting screens would have been out being used. There would be abandoned tools, fossils wrapped for transport. This place doesn't look like Carson re-opened it when he returned."

Mike gave another section a few sweeps with his brush. "And these fossils aren't anything special. Common low-level sea creatures. No big discovery to rush back here to exploit."

"We use the term *study*," Grant said.

"And I use the term *cash-on-delivery*," Mike said.

Grant climbed back up to ground level. A blast of cold air smacked him in the face. He surveyed the area. No indication Carson had set up camp here. But over the months this harsh environment would have scoured away the tents and folding tables that made up the usual campsite for an operation like this. Mike joined him.

"Looks like a long trip for nothing," Mike said.

"I was hoping there'd be some indication that at least he'd returned here. He may have never gotten back."

If this location came in as a dry hole, Grant didn't know how they'd get a lead on where Professor Carson might be. Grant was going to need to play the card he'd kept hidden up his sleeve.

"There's something else we can look for," Grant said. "A discovery he'd told me about in a letter. He'd kept it hidden for fear of the Chinese. It's nearby. Maybe he set up there."

"Worth a look."

Laoxin stepped up out of the pit. "Find anything?"

"Not yet. I want to go check out that dry creek bed to the west."

Laoxin shouted something to the guard. He turned and stepped over to the group.

"Go, go," Laoxin said to Grant.

Grant went into the dig and picked up two shovels from the stack. He returned and handed one to Mike.

"Merry Christmas," Grant said.

"Just what I always wanted. How did you know?"

Grant led the group around the crusty lakebed edge and then up the dried creek bed. The soil in it was much coarser, with stones washed down from the highlands littering the wash. They trudged uphill. Grant wished he had the coordinates with him to plug into Laoxin's GPS device. That would have pinpointed the specific location of the fossil Carson had written about. Instead, all Grant knew for sure was that it was in this wash.

Through all his field work, he'd trained himself to look for something different, a marker that shouted that this area, this strata, this coloration was dissimilar enough that it might harbor something interesting. He brought all that skill to bear.

Suddenly the location jumped out at him. To the left, a patch of earth was much sandier than the rest of the wash, with no larger rocks. Someone had dug this spot up, and then filled it back in.

"Over there," he said.

Mike smiled. "Oh, yeah."

"I do not understand," Laoxin said.

"Trust me," Grant said.

He and Mike stepped over to the spot and began to dig at opposite sides of the sandy patch of earth. The dirt shoveled easily, further proof that it had been recently returned to this spot, never compacted by the monsoon rain.

"Wait a minute," Mike said. "Isn't this the kind of stuff you bring grad students to do?"

It wasn't long before they both hit something hard. They shoveled slower and shallower. Soon they'd excavated a spot about three meters around and a half meter deep. They both knelt inside the little pit and swept the remaining sand away by hand.

"I'll be damned," Grant said.

The fossil beneath them was fully articulated, a rarity for any find. The creature was a quadruped, powerfully built, clearly a predator by the length of the claws and the long head with a jaw filled with jagged teeth. Incisors jutted down from the upper jaw, but pointed more forward than down, almost tusk-like. But the amazing part was the set of bat-like wings that sprouted from the back.

"There be dragons," Grant said.

"That cannot be real," Laoxin said.

"That's what people said about every species the first time someone found one," Grant said. He turned to Mike. "How do you think this rock's going to treat us?"

Mike smiled at the reference to their days in the college lab. "Probably going to be teaching hard lessons."

The structure was fascinating, with a dual clavicle supporting the front legs and the wings, and a bull-like neck to anchor all the muscles that made both move.

"And look at this," Mike said.

He bent down and pulled out his brush. He swept the sand from a section of the wing. Between the bones stretched a bumpy impression of the skin. Mike ran a finger across the surface.

"Like a *Tyrannosaur*," Grant said.

A tail coiled at the fossil's rear. A fan of small bones created a spade. Certain pterosaurs had a similar appendage, believed to help steering in flight.

"This throws a lot of science on its ear," Grant said.

"Yeah, it's worth a fortune."

The guard had been keeping watch down the wash. He glanced over his shoulder at the excavated fossil. His eyes went wide and he let fly a stream of high-pitched Chinese. Laoxin responded with what sounded like a harsh, condescending admonishment. Grant gave Mike a quizzical look.

"He said something about digging up a demon," Mike said.

"I had workers in the Amazon tell me the same thing once."

"How'd that work out?"

Grant remembered his recent terrifying encounter with the giant snake of the Aztec Viper King. "Perfectly. All myths put calmly to rest."

Something stuck up near the edge of the fossil. Grant ran his fingers over it and uncovered a bit of dark green leather. He dug a little more. The leather wrapped around a thin rectangular item. He unfolded the sheet and exposed a conventional school notebook. He flipped it open. The same cryptic shorthand Professor Carson had used years ago filled the pages.

"This is the fossil Professor Carson's letter described, and this is definitely his notebook. It must be the one he used for this find. He left it here so he wouldn't carry any clues about it away where someone might find them."

"Except for you," Laoxin said.

"Hand me that leather," Mike said.

Grant passed it over. Mike laid it down beside the fossilized wing. He rotated it about thirty degrees.

"Notice anything?"

The leather pattern matched the fossil wing.

"My God," Grant said. "Somewhere out there, things like this are still alive."

CHAPTER EIGHT

Grant paged through the notebook. Carson had made sketches of the fossilized…he hated to use the word…dragon.

"These are Carson's notes about this find," Grant said. "If he knew where its descendants were still roaming about, he'd have put it in here. That's why the letter he left me directed me to find the book."

"You can still read that nonsense?" Mike said.

"It's been twenty years. I'm kind of rusty. It will take me some time."

"We do that back at truck," Laoxin said. "This too exposed."

Grant had to agree. Out in this cold and wind he'd never concentrate.

"What about this find?" Mike said.

"We can't take it," Grant said.

"This is no time for the holier-than-thou discussion," Mike said. "We leave this here, and locals find it, it comes out in a hundred useless pieces, and you know it. We can get it out in one. I know a buyer who will make it well worth our while."

"Even if I agreed to join you on the Dark Side," Grant said, "which I won't, no way we have the tools or people to get this properly excavated. And we're here to find Professor Carson, not to collect specimens. It stays and we go. Let's rebury it."

Mike shook his head and began to shovel. In minutes they had the hole filled in. This time Grant spread some gravel and a few larger stones on top to make the location blend in better. As they made their way back to the truck, Grant noticed Mike paying close attention to the surrounding terrain, as if memorizing the details around this location. He couldn't help but think it was so Mike could find his way back later to plunder the find.

As they approached the truck, Laoxin shouted some commands to the guards and they took positions at the front and rear of the truck. She pointed at the cab.

"You go to work in there."

"With your people skills," Grant said, "have you considered a career in the field of correctional facility officer?"

Grant climbed up into the cab and turned on the dim overhead light. It was still cold, but being out of the wind made a big difference. He pulled a pencil and a notepad from his pocket. He remembered transcribing Carson's notes decades ago, and the long hours spent in the lab cleaning and cataloging finds. It had always been so exciting knowing he was the first human being to glimpse whatever fossil he was cleaning. That sense of excitement had never waned.

He began to unwind the professor's shorthand, picking out the Latin phrases, remembering the abbreviations Carson favored for common words. He was soon lost in solving the puzzle, and each sentence he unlocked just accelerated him into parsing the next.

The passenger door opened. Mike stuck his head in. "How you doing?"

"Good. Relax, I just started."

"Buddy, you've been at it for two hours."

Grant looked up at the sun. It had passed apogee.

"Damn," he said. "I have enough to get us moving. I can keep working on the rest."

He got out of the truck and headed for the tailgate. Mike paralleled him on the other side. Laoxin stood to one side at a slight modification of parade rest.

"This book is a gold mine," Grant said. "I only have some of it translated, but it's enough to get us going."

He opened the book to the first page where the sketches of the dinosaur/dragon appeared.

"So just like his letter to me described, he finds the skeleton on his own while his team works the main dig. He discovers the skull first, and the odd incisors and unfamiliar shape get him very excited about finding something wholly new. Day by day over the course of a week, he uncovers sections of it and then reburies the fossil, knowing that this area is outside his archeological permit and the Chinese might jail him and take the fossil. The sketch in the book was made one section at a time. We saw the whole fossil. He never did."

Mike shook his head. "The guy never ceases to amaze."

"Carson is certain that fossils like these inspired the whole Chinese mythos of dragons, especially when he takes a close look at the protruding incisors. They are hollow."

"Just like the pterodactyl beaks in your book," Mike said.

"You actually read it?"

"Every Nobel Prize-worthy word."

"Except that was a story," Grant said. "And no, these are hollow like hoses. He hypothesizes that they are either an extension of a sensory organ or, long shot, they expelled something."

"Something like fire," Laoxin said.

"Something like something," Grant said. "Plenty of animals expel things. Vipers spit venom. Skunks spray. Spiders shoot webs. If this creature did eject something, it may have been mythologized into fire at some point. Or maybe it really breathed fire."

Grant flipped to another page where Carson had laid out measurements of the skull and churned out a page of math underneath.

"Carson estimates a relatively big, developed brain in this creature. We know that man's evolution took a big leap forward when he mastered fire. Cooked food digested better and reduced disease. He hypothesizes that if dragons cooked their own food, boom, evolutionary explosion."

"Yet, no dragons in the world today," Mike said.

"Or are there?" Grant said. "Carson goes into town for supplies and comes across a travelling leather trader. He spies the section we discovered wrapped around the book. Having studied the fossilized skin in great detail, he knows that it's an unbelievable match. The trader says it is a rare skin considered most lucky to own. The translation from Chinese is wisdom skin."

"Dragons in Chinese culture are associated with wisdom," Laoxin said.

"So Carson asks the trader where he got it," Grant continued. "He says he purchased it in Szechuan province in a village called Zhōng Xiū."

"So in Szechuan province, there are still dragons," Laoxin said.

"That's what Carson believed. So he wrote that on his next trip back, he'll be going straight there to begin the search. What's that province like?"

"Quite developed in east, less so in west as terrain rises," Laoxin said. "Mountains heavily forested still. Anti-government sentiments run high, and the PLA not enter there in force, afraid of starting something they finish with tanks in streets."

"And those remote mountain forests are what Carson was looking for. Based on the stratum he found the fossil, the area of Inner Mongolia we're in now most closely resembled western Szechuan province in this fossil's era. The leather section and the story from the trader convinced Carson the species may still survive."

"Then Carson in Szechuan," Laoxin said. "We go back to plane and go now."

CHAPTER NINE

Two more seats were filled on the plane for this next trip. Both guards and their protective weaponry came along for the ride. Grant thought it exceptionally disconcerting to have assault rifles and hand grenades in an aircraft cabin. The two guards looked at each other, then all about the cabin with nervous glances throughout the trip. They grabbed their seats in fear every time turbulence nudged the plane.

"I don't think they're frequent fliers," Grant said.

"No, from the looks of them, they're Mongolian locals," Mike said. "Probably never been more than a hundred miles from where they were born. Hired out from a local gang leader."

"Coincidental that you know the type," Grant said.

"We all can't travel to digs sponsored by public grants. I work on commission and I have to take some shortcuts."

Grant was about to dig into him about those shortcuts hurting the science but stopped himself. Finding Professor Carson was the priority.

"Those two guards really stink," he said.

"They weren't hired for their hygiene," Mike said.

Laoxin returned from talking with the pilot and stood between them. "We land at Xinjin Airport, outside Chengdu. That place us close to Zhōng Xiū, where Carson went, but bypass major airport."

"For a totalitarian regime, we seem to be able to avoid the Chinese authorities pretty well."

"That is what I am paid to do. But once on ground, you two attract much attention. Westerners not common. Truck will be waiting. You hurry into back and stay covered. We drive from there up into mountains, to village Carson describe."

"Is there cell service that far into the mountains?"

"Not likely."

Grant was relieved. "Then maybe we'll find him there doing research, simply out of touch with the world."

"Also not likely."

"I'm beginning to think that 'Laoxin' translates to 'rain cloud' in Chinese. Let's go for some positivity here."

A half hour later, the plane approached Chengdu. Out the window spread a great, sprawling city, stretching to the horizon through the ever-present Chinese brown haze. The large international airport passed by on the left, and the plane angled for a much smaller airfield and runway ahead. Unlike their last destination, this one had small planes parked on the apron and a few hangars.

They landed and taxied off the runway to a location far from the rest of the airport buildings. The plane stopped and Laoxin opened the door and dropped the stairs. Much warmer air than in Inner Mongolia filled the plane, as did an omnipresent smell of partially burned diesel fuel and something tangy enough to be airborne metals. Grant promised himself to look up and thank every Congressman who voted for the Clean Air Act in the 1970s.

Laoxin looked around outside then pulled her head back in.

"Car waiting outside. Get in and stay down."

Grant grabbed his bag and Mike shouldered his rucksack and picked up the green duffel bag.

"What's in that?" Grant said.

"Tools of the trade. Just because you head out across the world half-prepared and dragging around tourist luggage doesn't mean that everyone does."

Two white Range Rover knock-offs sat at the edge of the taxiway with doors and tailgates open. Air snorkels and brush guards promised that the mud-splattered vehicles were ready to tackle the interior mountains.

Grant practically stumbled down the steps balancing the weight of his bag. In his mind he envisioned saving face with a Tom Cruise-like sprint to the waiting truck. But once on the tarmac, the best he could manage was a Kevin James-inspired trot dragging the rollaboard behind him. Both wheels made embarrassing, squeaky chirps.

Mike sprinted past him and tossed both his bags into the trailing SUV cargo area as if they were weightless. He jumped into the backseat and slunk down.

Grant finally made it to the truck and heaved his bag in beside Mike's. He joined his old friend in the back seat.

"There's a disguise in here for you," Mike said.

He passed Grant a wide-brimmed straw coolie hat.

"Sure," Grant said. "Add a pair of sunglasses and I could walk right into the office of the Party Chairman like I owned the place."

One of the guards climbed into the driver's seat and wedged his rifle down against the console. Laoxin and the other guard got into the lead vehicle. Seconds later both vehicles were on their way and out of the airport.

In a few turns, the trucks were on a major highway, wedged into traffic that moved at a steady pace. Grant shielded his face with the hat and peeped up over the edge of the door like a periscope. A little kid stared at him from the back seat of a car pacing theirs. Grant ducked back down.

"Stay down," Mike said. "Curiosity gets you in trouble in this kind of business."

"Curiosity is what got me into the *legitimate* side of this business to begin with. Kind of hard to keep it in check."

"Buddy, you've given me some serious condemnation from minute number one. Haven't seen each other in decades and you talk to me like I'm a serial killer."

Now that he mentioned it, Grant did think of someone who plundered fossil after fossil without any gain to science a type of serial killer. "This isn't the place to discuss this," he said instead.

"Actually, it's perfect. Nice and tight with an audience that doesn't speak English."

"Fine. We graduated and you threw away a career opportunity for fossil piracy. The last semester…"

"You want to bring up those bogus theft charges again?"

"Those mammoth femurs didn't walk out of lab storage on their own," Grant said.

"And I didn't steal them. But everyone sure assumed I did. Even after the investigating board decided not to charge me."

"Lack of evidence is different than lack of guilt."

"Which is why I decided to track them down on my own. I discovered the person who had motive and opportunity. Who it was isn't important after all these years, but I confronted her and she confessed. I didn't care about turning her in. I wanted to find the man who ordered the theft and get back the fossils. But by the time I tracked him down, the femurs were long gone."

"And this shadowy fossil pillager wasn't upset you found him?"

"Just the opposite. He appreciated my resourcefulness. I told him I wouldn't steal anything for him. He said he wouldn't ask me to. There were plenty more fossils out there to be found and sold."

"So that's how you met Angelo Destro. Then you jumped at joining the black market, the kind of money-for-hire job you'd always wanted."

"I'd have been happy staying legitimate. But the stigma of the theft charges was going to hang over me forever. Your attitude is proof of that. I'd never teach or be trusted enough to be recruited for field research. So, I signed up with him. And I've done alright."

"So, you came on this expedition to see what trinkets you might pick up in China?"

"No. I signed up here after getting contacted by Carson's wife through Laoxin. In this business, you might do alright but eventually you have to admit that you haven't done *all right.* This looked like a chance to rack up points in a different column for once. Carson was a decent guy."

"Let's keep him in the present tense and say he still is a decent guy."

"I'm good with that." He sighed. "I spent decades collecting outside the rules. I know Carson was disappointed in me, in my choices. We hadn't spoken since the theft charges were dropped. But hearing he'd gone missing reminded me of where I was, and where we were when we were studying under him. Maybe I thought I owed him. Maybe I wanted redemption. Whatever the reason, I'm here, and definitely not as a treasure hunter."

Grant was going to have to mull this over. Maybe Mike had gotten a bad rap over the lab thefts. Maybe he was turning over a new leaf, rescuing Carson to atone for his sins. He'd liked Mike throughout their college years. He sure wanted his old friend's story to be true.

If it wasn't, this expedition would be even harder.

CHAPTER TEN

After a while, the truck seemed to be driving much faster. Grant hazarded another peek through the window. Traffic was down to almost nothing. Through the front windshield he could see tall, green mountains rising up ahead. Clouds hung like a shroud around the peaks. The sun had dipped below the clouds to create an early dusk.

"I think we're getting close," he said.

Mike popped up and looked around. "The Kunlun mountain range. Wild and wooly up in there. Thick forests up to the tree lines, clouds most of the time above that. Smuggling routes galore out of China."

Grant gave him a disappointed look.

"Or so I've heard," Mike added.

The superhighway shed several lanes, then several more, then entered the mountain range as a two lane through a narrow, twisting valley. Forests blanketed the steep slopes that rose on both sides. Deep shadows cloaked the road and both SUVs turned on their headlights.

The driver appeared unaware that the road conditions had changed, and seemed to still be travelling at superhighway speeds. The high SUV leaned around each curve as the driver seemed physically unable to move his foot from the gas to the brake. Grant gripped the back of the seat in terror.

"These drivers do this all the time," Mike said. "Gotta trust them."

The truck roared around a curve. Another vehicle missed sideswiping them by millimeters in the oncoming lane. The driver steered the SUV to hug the guardrail. A missing section zoomed by. Grant looked down to see a crushed cargo truck twenty meters downhill.

"Not able to embrace the trust the driver thing," Grant said.

A harrowing hour later, the brake lights of the lead SUV flashed a merciful red and the truck pulled into the small village of Zhōng Xiū. Most of the walls of the tight-packed buildings were fashioned from local brownish rocks, some from hand-hewn grey blocks. Nothing looked like it had been built in the last century. Moss and black algae spotted the low, tiled roofs. The corners of each roof hosted a stone gargoyle. And while the buildings were a hodgepodge of sizes, shapes and styles, these corner ornaments were not. They were all dragons.

The SUVs stopped in front of a building that looked like a store.

"This looks like the place Carson described where the trader bought that leather," Grant said.

"Well, we can't hide our Western faces anymore," Mike said. "Out we go."

They got out of the SUV. Laoxin still sat in hers. She waved them closer and they went to her window.

"Shop keeper inside is Carson's contact. You two go ask for him. Westerner looking for Westerner is normal. Chinese looking for Westerner is suspicious. Then shopkeeper lie and deny everything."

"Makes sense," Mike said.

"You know enough Chinese to do that?" Grant said.

"Sure. The guy will think he's talking to a three-year-old, but we'll be able to communicate."

Grant hoped if they couldn't, then Laoxin could at least step in as a translator before the shopkeeper sent them out in the wrong direction.

They entered the shop. The store was redolent of a myriad of spices, all arrayed in containers along a wall behind a counter. The shelves were half-filled with cans and boxes of food, only some of which Grant could make sense of. Other shelves looked like they held basics like light bulbs and nails and coils of rope. Given the hair-raising trip back to civilization along the narrow road, this place had to be the go-to shop for everything.

A wizened little man with thick glasses and sparse gray hair shuffled up to the counter.

"Can I help you?" he said.

"English!" Grant said with relief.

"For Westerners traveling alone. My father learned from Allied soldiers on the Burma Road. He taught me."

"I'm Grant Coleman. This is Mike Rabon."

"Lin Zhong, at your service."

"We are paleontologists looking for a friend who might have contacted you a few months ago. A tall man named Carson. He'd found a swath of wisdom skin."

The old man's eyes narrowed. "How many people know of this skin?"

"As far as we know, Professor Carson and us."

"That is already three too many." Zhong smacked the counter with his palm. "A trader stole the skin from me when I refused to sell it. And I refused because some secrets need to be kept. Now the secret is out."

"Is the skin from…" Mike paused.

"Say it," Grant said.

"It sounds ridiculous."

"It is from the dragons on the mountain," the old man said.

"See," Grant said. "Not ridiculous at all. Of course, being Chinese helps him sell it."

"The mountain is called *Huǒ Lin*. Forest of Fire. For generations our families know not to set foot there. Dragons let no one pass. Hundreds of years ago, one warlord tried to conquer the dragons, built a fortress to claim the land. His force was destroyed. Since then, the mountain has been off limits. Even in times of starvation, or to escape the Cultural Revolution, people would die a known death before facing the unknown death on the mountain."

"Then how did someone get the skin?" Mike asked.

"Sometimes a dragon dies, falls off a cliff, washes down the mountainside. We find the carcass. We destroy it to make certain the secret stays hidden. One villager could not resist the temptation to sell wisdom skin for the great sums it would bring. We stopped him before it was too late. The trader came across the piece used as evidence in those proceedings."

"Dragons are a hard secret to keep," Grant said.

"The world has a balance among all species," the old man said. "Man upsets that by demanding too much space. And so we lose the snow leopard, the panda, the tiger. We are in balance with the dragons, neither crossing the boundary of the other. We keep the secret of its existence knowing the government would never allow the balance to remain. They would seek to exploit the dragon. The dragon would not stand for that."

"So Carson came to you looking for the dragons?"

"And I explained to him what I explain to you now. He agreed to stop his search and return to Chengdu in the morning. But when dawn came, he was gone. He'd headed up the mountain, and did not return."

"But you don't know he died up there?"

"I only know that in my lifetime, no one has ever returned. Not even the local people who know how to live off the land and navigate the forest. A Western professor would be dragon food the first day."

Grant pulled Mike away to the edge of the shop. "He might still be alive."

"After months? The old man couldn't live off the land in Yellowstone, let alone in dragon-infested China."

"We've come this far," Grant said, "and all the proof there is of dragons are stories and the scrap of leather in your pocket, and that might be from a *Komodo* dragon for all we know."

"Even if the dragon thing is all mythology, there are still a dozen real, lethal animals that patrol that forest. Tigers, snakes, plenty more. We now have a witness that Carson walked in and didn't walk out. That's not much to risk our lives on. In my business you learn the balance of acceptable risk and probable payout. This doesn't balance."

"Let's talk this over outside," Grant said. He turned to the shopkeeper. "Thank you, sir."

"Go home," he said. "Save your lives."

The two left the shop. Laoxin stood leaning against the door of her SUV. The guards sat in the trucks. She straightened up as they approached.

"What does the old man say?" she said.

"He thinks there's a mountain full of dragons," Grant said. "And he's certain that Carson went to climb it."

"Excellent," Laoxin said.

Diesel engines roared unseen from both ends of the street. A military truck appeared and stopped behind Grant's SUV. Another rolled in from the other side of the street and parked nose-to nose with Laoxin's. Soldiers dismounted from each. They carried full packs and wore combat helmets and bandoleers of ammunition. They pointed their rifles at the three of them. Grant's pulse went into overdrive.

The sergeant barked a series of commands in Chinese. Grant had no idea what he was saying, but raising his hands in surrender seemed like a safe bet as a response. Mike followed suit.

The sergeant saw Laoxin and straightened up. He raised one hand to his brow in a salute.

Laoxin went to attention and returned his salute. The sergeant said a few curt words and Laoxin responded.

"I have a bad feeling she never quit the PLA," Grant said.

"Thank you for your assistance," she said to Grant and Mike. "You now under protection of People's Liberation Army. Provide full cooperation and you will be treated well."

"Cooperation doing what?" Mike said. Unbridled fury raged in his eyes.

"What you come here to do," she said. "Hunt a dragon."

CHAPTER ELEVEN

Zhong's granddaughter, Changying, burst out of the room in the back of the shop. She was in her mid-twenties. Her clothes were dirty from unloading boxes in the back, though she'd obviously taken a break to eavesdrop on her grandfather. She threw her long hair over her shoulder and gave her grandfather an angry, admonishing look.

"Why were you even talking to those foreigners?" She rushed to the front window and glanced out through the curtains.

"They were looking for that professor," he said. "I could not let them follow him and die on the mountain as well."

Changying gave him an angry look. "Foolish old man. Now people have seen you with those foreigners. They should not be out here without a government guide any more than that other professor should have been. You are just begging for the police to drag you out and off for questioning."

"All I told them was to warn them away, to keep them off our mountain, to keep our secrets safe. Wise people would go back home."

"Americans are never wise. They will want to search the mountain even more now." She looked out the window again. "Damn it. Soldiers. A lot of them. The American have their hands in the air."

"Now this is much worse," Zhong said. "The soldiers will force them up into the mountains in search of all our secrets."

Changying rushed from the window and began to push Zhong to the rear of the store.

"Get out of here! They will be in for you next. I'll tell them I could not speak English, did not understand them."

"They won't believe you. No, I can't run away from this. They will take those men and go looking for the missing professor, and for the dragons of the Forest of Fire. They will want to take a local guide as well. It might as well be me."

"You can't go climb the mountain at your age."

"No, I couldn't climb the mountain at *your* age. But I can at mine. Walking the Forest of Fire requires wisdom more than strength."

A PLA sergeant burst in through the door, rifle at the ready.

"Okay, which one of you was talking with the foreigners?"

Changying went to raise her hand. Zhong held it down.

"That would be me," Zhong said. "They came looking after an American professor who had been in here weeks ago, then went up into the Forest of Fire."

The sergeant looked around the store. "You sell supplies for that kind of trip. You know about the Forest of Fire?"

"As much as anyone in the village."

The sergeant stepped over and grabbed his arm. It was like being bound in steel.

"You are coming with me." The sergeant turned to Changying. "We have the old man with us. Any problems in this village while he's gone, and he will not come back."

***

Outside the shop, Grant looked at Laoxin with disgust.

"I can't believe I trusted her," he said to Mike. "And I really can't believe you did."

"Me?"

"You're used to working with double-dealers. Don't you have some kind of radar for that thing by now?"

"Oh, she tripped it. But she was our ticket in here. Figured I'd ride the wave, see how it broke."

"You could have at least—"

A crashing noise cut him off. From behind them, Lin Zhong flew out of the shop, nearly losing his footing. The PLA sergeant stepped out and gave the old man an extra shove with his rifle to get him between Mike and Grant. He hurled some kind of insult at the trembling old man. Then he and Laoxin exchanged a few sentences.

"Zhong!" Grant said. "Did us talking to you get you dragged out here?"

"No," he said. "I did it to myself. They were going to take someone anyway."

"She's convinced we'll find dragons in the Forest of Fire."

"She is right," Zhong said. "And the dragons will kill us for our trouble."

CHAPTER TWELVE

"You lied to Maxwell Carson's widow to get on this trip?" Grant said.

For the first time, Laoxin laughed. Its evil tone gave Grant a chill.

"Carson widow not put trip together. All Chinese government. You ever talk to widow?"

Grant looked at Mike. They both shook their heads.

"Damn it," Mike said under his breath.

"Spy tell us Carson find dragon fossil before he leaves, possible link to dragons still living. We wait for him to return to excavation on return trip. He does not come back to excavation. Instead disappears. We find Carson letter to Professor Coleman. But the coordinates of the hidden fossil make no sense. So we recruit two protégées who can track down former mentor. Let them translate fossil location, and now the book. Plan is perfect."

"We're United States citizens," Grant said. "You can't just kidnap us without repercussions."

"You are two illegal aliens," Laoxin said. "Sneak into China. Probably CIA spies. If your situation become public knowledge, you go into PLA prison. Never come out."

That sounded like a living hell.

"I'm willing to keep this all between us," Grant said. "You go your way, we'll go ours. We post a nice review on travel sites."

"Your way. My way. Same way. Up mountain."

"What do you need us for now? We got you to where the dragons are supposed to be."

"Dinosaur experts might be handy."

"Why do you need Zhong? You can let him go."

"Hostage to keep the village quiet. Mission secret until complete."

A soldier stepped forward and gave Grant and Mike a shove toward the SUV where the tailgate stood open. Grant grabbed his rollaboard, Mike his rucksack. Mike reached for the green duffel bag. A shout from the soldier and a jab with a rifle barrel indicated that was a bad idea. Mike stepped back without the duffel bag.

Then Laoxin spoke rapid-fire to the thugs who had accompanied them from the airport. They nodded, entered the SUVs, and drove away. Minutes ago, Grant couldn't wait to get out of the SUV driven by the ape from the dig site. Now he wished he was in there with him.

Grant felt like an idiot standing beside his vacation luggage while surrounded by a squad of soldiers in the middle of nowhere. But he wasn't going to leave everything he owned behind. With great embarrassment, he extended the bag's handle and gripped the end. Mike gave the bag a dismissive look.

"I know," Grant said. "I should have valet-checked the suitcase to the mountain top."

***

Laoxin stepped away from the group and into the shadowed alley beside Zhong's shop. Empty crates and boxes littered the space. She pulled her satellite phone from her pocket and dialed the number of her commander. She knew he'd be waiting on her call. He answered on the first ring.

"What is your status?" he said.

Her commander never wasted words or time.

"I've confirmed where Professor Carson went hunting for dragons, and that the wisdom skin he found is dragon skin."

"So, this wild story you're chasing may actually be true."

She wanted to shout at him that of course it was true. If she hadn't thought it was true, she would never have proposed the mission.

"Yes, it seems so."

"I'm going to tell the party hierarchy what you've promised to deliver, so now you'd better come through."

"I will. A larger force on the ground would have made it easier."

"And stir up the locals? They are still simmering over some counter-revolutionaries we sent to prison last year. We don't need more protestors waving signs and throwing fire bombs. Plus, a larger force might draw international attention. They would assume it's for internal security, but when they find out it's because we discovered dragons, then the eco-crazy pressure will come worldwide. We already put up with enough crap about snow leopards."

Laoxin didn't think she could have gotten more help, but at least she gave it a try.

"The other support you requested will be standing by for your call. But if I don't hear from you in two days, my faith and patience will be tested."

"Understood."

Her commander hung up. Laoxin cursed and kicked an empty wooden crate down the alley.

The Party moved too slowly about everything. Unrest wasn't crushed quickly enough. Traitors weren't imprisoned long enough. And opportunities weren't seized even when they were hanging inches from people's noses.

The story Laoxin had told Grant about her past was all fiction. She had been born in a dirt-poor failing commune so far from any city that even electricity was miles away. She had hated everything about it and had enlisted in the PLA to step out of that hell and to step up into a position of power. Her goal was to never go back home again.

It soon became apparent to her that it took more than just good performance to get ahead. You had to make a splash, make a name for yourself to be recognized and get into the fast track that brought power and wealth along with your rank.

Her family had lived in Chengdu before the Cultural Revolution had forcibly relocated them to living hell in the country. They'd told stories of the Forest of Fire and the dragons that lived there. As a child, Laoxin had dreamed of seeing one. As an adult, she'd dreamed of capturing one and using it as her ticket to riches. When her contacts told her about Professor Carson and his dragon quest, she uncovered enough corroborating facts to convince herself that he'd been on to something.

Convincing others in power had been much more difficult.

In the end she'd been assigned a smaller force than she'd wanted, more lightly armed than needed, and it was made up of some seriously second-rate soldiers. But she thought overall the squads she commanded might end up being just enough. The two Americans she had duped into helping out had made her job much easier.

There would still be bumps along the road ahead. Some of the soldiers would probably die. She might have to burn this flyspeck village down if the villagers' cooperation wasn't forthcoming enough. The two Americans certainly couldn't be allowed to live to tell the world their role in the dragon capture. As the Americans say, you have to break eggs to make an omelet.

And if all went as she planned, when this was over, her short-sighted current commander would be reporting to her. She'd relish that.

She put the satellite phone away and started back for her team in the village. It was time to go capture a dragon.

***

Foreboding filled Grant as he watched Laoxin assign half the soldiers to stay in the village. That meant only half as many on the dragon hunt. It also meant that their oppressive boot heels would be at the villagers' throats while the hunting party was gone.

The soldiers heading out on the hunt herded Mike, Grant, and Zhong through the village. Laoxin took the lead along the narrow, uphill street.

"You're going to surprise me," Grant whispered to Mike, "with a flamethrower in that rucksack to get us out of this, right?"

"Rule #1 in secret foreign jobs," Mike said. "Let the locals carry the guns. Fewer law enforcement issues."

"Ah, the good old days when a law enforcement issue was the biggest problem to have."

"Hey, buddy, I know this trip has turned into a visit to hell. Whatever you think of me or the life I've led, know that I've got your back out here. We'll get through this together."

Grant saw a bit of the old Mike he'd spent hours in the college paleontology lab with. Maybe there was still part of that man inside Mike trying to resurface. Grant sure hoped so.

The village ended at two tiers of rice patties. Beyond that loomed the mountain and the dark forest that filled its flank. A narrow trail entered the woods.

Laoxin raised a hand and the column stopped. She shouted some orders and five soldiers moved to the front of the line. The rest began loading weapons and tightening pack straps.

"What's the point of killing the dragon anyway?" Grant said.

"They're not going to kill it."

Mike pointed to the end of the group. Using a wireless controller, the last soldier in line maneuvered a narrow, motorized cart on ATV tires. The cart carried lengths of cargo cables and a giant folded cargo net.

"They're going to bring it back alive."

"Haven't they seen, oh, *every* dinosaur movie ever made? That idea never ends well. Why would they do that?"

"Revenue," Mike said. "Do you know how much they make leasing out pandas all over the world? Word in my circles is the panda program is in trouble. Too much inbreeding. Too many birth defects. Something has to replace that program. Enter the dragon."

"Fifteen soldiers. One dragon. I'd boost those odds."

"A small force," Zhong said "means that there is some secrecy about Laoxin's mission. The PLA prefers strength in numbers."

"Secret sounds bad," Grant said.

"People do desperate things to keep secrets," Zhong said. "And that is always bad."

CHAPTER THIRTEEN

Laoxin shouted another order and the group moved forward into the forest. Grant, Mike, and Zhong were in the middle of the group, eliminating any possibility of slipping away unnoticed.

For hours, the group trudged on. Despite the reasonable temperatures, Grant sweated up a tropical storm. He'd quickly given up trying to pull his rollaboard over the dirt and roots and kept switching it from hand to hand as one shoulder or the other began to ache under the strain.

Enormous trees spread their branches overhead into an interlocking mesh of leaves that blocked the sun. Bamboo grew in the few patches where light broke through small gaps in the canopy. Some of the tree trunks spread wider than a giant sequoia.

"Can you imagine how old some of these trees must be?" Grant said.

"Legends say they grow for a thousand years," Zhong said. "No one enters the forest to harvest them."

The soldiers had started out the trek along the narrow game trail wary and quiet. But after hours of no contact with anything larger than an insect, Grant could feel that the tension among the men had subsided. He had a chance to study them closer as well. This was no elite military force. Some had shaggy hair, most were unshaven. Bad teeth seemed to have been an enlistment pre-requisite. This group wasn't as outlaw-scary as the guards from the fossil dig site, more a collection of conscripted peasant farmers. The condition of their uniforms and gear, and the obedience they displayed to the sergeant and Laoxin were the only confirmation that they were actually soldiers.

The lead soldier stopped and held up one hand. The group halted and dropped to one knee.

Grant's pulse sped up. Scientific discoveries be damned. He did not want to meet a dragon in the forest right now. Or ever.

The soldier studied the woods around him, listened, then gave the rest of the group a thumbs up.

Before the others could rise, a black and orange blur charged out of the bushes. The huge tiger easily weighed over 250 kilos, more than twice its soldier prey. It hit the man in the chest paws first and drove him to the ground. A single killing bite to the neck and the soldier went limp.

The rest of the soldiers recovered from the shock. Rifles turned in the direction of the tiger.

The tiger wasn't about to wait around for retribution. It bounded away into the brush, dragging the dead soldier by the neck as the body trailed back under the tiger's belly.

The rest of the squad opened fire and the boom of rifle shots split the air. Grant ducked on instinct. Bullets ripped through leaves and sent splinters flying from tree trunks.

But the tiger was long gone.

The sergeant shouted at the men and they stopped firing. He walked up the line and slapped men in the helmets as he screamed at them.

"He says they are worthless," Zhong said. "Scared of cats in the woods."

"Count me as scared when the cats are like that," Grant said. "Record my vote for turning back."

Laoxin joined in the verbal abuse and ordered the soldiers up and on their feet. The second-now-first soldier in line headed up the trail. His face was white and his rifle shook a bit in his hands.

"Doesn't look like your vote counts," Mike said to Grant.

They advanced up the trail. At the scene of the tiger attack, fresh blood glistened on the broken leaves that littered the ground. The soldier ahead of Grant scooped up the dead man's dropped rifle.

"If they can't defend themselves against a tiger," Grant said, "God help us if we really do find a dragon."

The path they tread soon widened enough for the men to pass easily. Which meant the animals that had made this part of the trail were bigger than the men were. Grant didn't like that revelation at all.

As the darkness neared absolute, the group stopped beside a wide stand of bamboo. Laoxin barked out some commands. The soldiers dropped in place and unshouldered their packs. Laoxin approached Grant and the others.

"We spend night here. Soldiers on guard for your protection."

"To protect us from escaping," Grant said.

"Knowing dragons in the forest enough to keep a wise man from escaping," Laoxin said. "Tomorrow we capture dragons."

Two of the soldiers unsheathed machetes and went to work on the circular stand of bamboo. In short order they'd cleared an area for the group to sleep among the stubble. The expedition moved into the space. Two soldiers took up guard positions at the perimeter. Within minutes, several tiny campfires began to burn and soldiers heated up rations.

Grant unzipped his rollaboard to display an embarrassing array of belongings. Pyjamas. A sleep mask. Slippers. He'd planned on being on a "first-class" expedition, sleeping in a hotel room with turndown service.

For food, he had a few protein bars and a bottle of water. He'd pack that as airplane snack food. Mike pulled a pouch of some kind of freeze-dried food from his bag.

"You look better prepared for roughing it than I am," Grant said.

"Rule #2," Mike said. "Plan to not starve."

"I'm getting a list of your rules when this adventure is over."

Grant passed a protein bar over to Zhong. He nodded in appreciation and ripped open the wrapper.

"Laoxin thinks we're dragon experts," Grant said.

"If we want her to keep us alive," Mike said, "we need to convince her that she's right."

CHAPTER FOURTEEN

After sunset, the air chilled quickly. The soldiers set up a larger fire in the center of the bamboo clearing and all gravitated closer to it for warmth. Insects chirped and buzzed from the black abyss outside the fire's circle of light. The three captives huddled beside their own smaller fire. Leaves snapped and crackled in the flames.

"They will see this fire from the village," Zhong said. "They will take it as a sign I am well."

"Sure they won't think it's a fire-breathing dragon?" Grant said.

"No, dragons just make flashes."

"What? I was just joking."

"It is how we are certain the dragons stalk the mountain," Zhong said. "How the forest got its name. We see the flashes of fire from the mountain at night. Not wildfires, just flares, like the striking and extinguishing of a single, huge match."

"How's an animal going to actually breathe fire without incinerating itself?" Mike said.

"Those tusk-like things might do it. Two tubes attached to some gland inside the head."

"Kind of moving into jackalope territory there, Grant."

"There's no denying the tusks do something."

"More likely they sing through the tubes to attract a mate."

"The good news about this paleontological debate is that, unlike most, we'll be able to solve it. The bad news is it might be the last thing we ever do."

"Zhong," Mike said. "Where do you see those flashes on the mountain?"

"Up high above the tree line. Mostly in the clouds."

"We're supposed to be dragon experts, so that will be our first piece of expertise. Dragons live above the tree line."

"Unless villagers are just seeing cloud-to-cloud lightning," Mike said.

"But the hypothesis makes sense," Grant said. "A winged predator would not evolve in a densely wooded area like this."

Out in the dark forest, a thick branch snapped.

"Which leaves this biome wide open for other predators," Grant added.

One of the soldiers made a cautious advance to the three men. He looked far too young to be in the military. His large, round glasses gave him an inadvert look of wonder. He managed a sheepish smile.

"This kid looks like he got separated from his school field trip and ended up here," Mike said.

The soldier went straight for Mike. He looked around to see that none of his comrades were looking, then bent down.

"Americans, no?" he whispered. "I know little English. My brother in college in California."

His brother's status seemed like an immense source of pride for the kid. He smiled with a mouth full of crooked teeth.

"And you're kidnapping people with the PLA," Mike said. "You sure got the short end of the family stick."

"Mike!" Grant said.

"He doesn't understand me," Mike said.

Since the boy was still smiling, it seemed that he hadn't.

Mike pointed at himself. "I am Mike." He pointed at the soldier. "You?"

"Tong," he said pointing to himself.

Another soldier from across the clearing shouted at Tong. He straightened up and the smile melted from his face. He pointed his rifle at Mike and said something curt in Chinese. Then he winked.

"Go USA!" he whispered.

He ran off back to the perimeter.

"Well, you made a friend," Grant said. "You two should grab a coffee together later."

Another, larger branch broke in the forest. A cry of alarm arose from the soldiers. They stood and weapons clicked as rounds loaded into chambers.

The guard closest to where the noise had happened flicked on a flashlight. Pointing it along with his rifle, he swept the beam across the darkness. It briefly lit some low scrub and tree trunks along the edge of the clearing as it passed.

The soldier crept forwards, each step almost silent as he moved closer to the trees. Ahead of him, the branches of a bush moved. He snapped the rifle to his shoulder and took aim. Soldiers around the fire shouted admonishments Grant did not comprehend.

A rabbit burst from the base of the bush. It charged the soldier and ran right between his legs. Then it made an almost ninety degree turn and barreled down the animal trail and into the darkness.

The startled soldier shouted a curse. The other soldiers started laughing. The victim of the rabbit charge turned around and gave them an angry look. Then he realized how ridiculous the situation was and joined in the laughter.

Above and behind him, a reptilian head three meters long materialized out of the darkness. Its long, crocodilian mouth opened and the firelight glittered off twin rows of dagger shaped teeth. The head darted down and clamped its jaws around the soldier. His top half vanished into the creature's mouth. The jaws closed with the crunch of bones. Blood spurted from the sides of the creature's mouth. The lizard head disappeared back into the dark and the lower half of the soldier dropped to the ground.

The soldiers screamed. Rifles opened fire and a hail of bullets cut through the air where the lizard head had been. Branches exploded and spun down to the ground.

Further away, larger branches cracked as the creature retreated. But the creature made no cry or roar. None of the bullets seemed to have hit their mark.

The soldiers paused to reload. Grant, Mike, and Zhong scrambled back to the perceived safety of the brighter fires in the center of the ring of armed men. Laoxin shouted for them to be still and listen.

"See!" Zhong said. "Dragons are coming to kill us all for trespassing."

"Damn," Mike said. "Grant, have you ever seen anything like that?"

"Funny you should ask," Grant said. But he stopped his answer there. A half dozen monsters had tried to kill him during three different expeditions. Now wasn't the time to list the casting call of giant creatures that seemed to be waiting for him every time he ventured from campus.

"Even with all that firing," Mike said, "they didn't seem like they hit it."

"It's like Star Wars storm troopers taught marksmanship to the PLA," Grant said.

From close in the forest came the sound of more branches breaking, this time from uphill. Nervous soldiers pointed their wavering rifles in that direction.

The giant lizard burst from the trees. Its eyes glowed orange and it let loose a roar like a lion. It stood three meters tall on four legs, solid muscle under leathery skin. The complete build was hard to see in the dark. But the white teeth in its gaping jaws were not.

The men opened fire again. A hailstorm of bullets flew at the animal. With a sharp swing of its head, it swept the nearest soldier off his feet and sent him sailing into the woods.

Then the creature screamed, not in anger this time but in pain. At least some of the bullets were hitting their mark. The animal bounded away uphill. A mass of branches snapped and leaves crushed in the forest beyond, then the woods went silent again. In a moment, insects buzzed anew.

The soldiers reloaded and kept their guns trained at the last place they'd seen the creature. The soldier who'd been thrown into the woods came staggering back. His left arm flapped limp against his side.

"This is unbelievable," Mike said.

"I remember when I used to be able to say that," Grant said.

Tong began to tend to the soldier who'd returned from the woods. His arm looked broken.

"We can hurt it," Mike said. "At least drive it back if it attacks again."

Zhong shook his head. "You talk like only one dragon lives in the Forest of Fire."

CHAPTER FIFTEEN

The rest of the night dragged by, with Grant only catching moments of exhausted sleep. Random noises awakened him and he hurriedly put on his glasses only to see that no new threat had entered the camp. The soldiers did not seem to sleep at all. Every sound from the woods sparked a cry of alarm and the aiming of rifles in that direction. Only Laoxin's rebukes kept the soldiers from spending the night firing at nothing.

The chill of the darkness worked its way into Grant's bones. With no one willing to risk entering the forest for fuel, the central fire had burned down to embers. The cold air seemed to take up permanent residence between the layers of Grant's clothes. Being overweight didn't even offer an advantage in heat conservation. He really needed to look into getting in better shape when he got home.

Dawn broke early since they were part of the way up the mountain, though the sun only penetrated the canopy in patches. But it was soon light enough to see the damage the creature had done during its attack. Smaller branches on the side where the animal had eaten the soldier were snapped and broken. The soldier's half-corpse still lay on the ground in a hardened puddle of dried blood. A cloud of flies hovered over it.

Uphill, where the creature had made its second attack, the damage was much worse. Smaller bushes had been trampled flat. Large branches hung at odd angles where the animal had broken them near the tree trunk. Bamboo leaves near the ground had a reddish tinge, which Grant attributed to fall coloration, until he realized it was the animal's blood.

Two soldiers approached Mike and Grant. They motioned with their rifles and some clipped Chinese that they needed to get up. Grant and Mike looked at each other, then complied. Laoxin joined them.

"Dragon expert go find dragon," she said.

"Out there?" Grant said. "Why go looking for that thing when it seemed to have no trouble finding us? I'm willing to wait for a next encounter. Play hard to get."

"Scout trail while soldiers prepare. Go now."

One of the soldiers prodded Grant in the ribs with the barrel of his rifle. The snarl on his face said he wasn't going to take no for an answer.

"Okay," Grant said. "Since you're asking nicely."

He stepped toward the area of the last attack. Mike moved to join him. The second soldier stepped in front of him and shoved him back.

"What the hell?" Mike said.

"Only one dragon expert," Laoxin said. "Both not die at once."

"We wouldn't want that," Grant said.

Zhong stepped forward. "I will go with you." He turned and made a curt bow to Laoxin. "With permission. I am more familiar with the plants and wildlife. I will translate for your soldier."

Laoxin considered it. "Go. You are hostage for your village. Village hostage for you also. Try to escape and they pay."

The soldier motioned for Grant to get moving. He and Zhong headed for the blood-splattered bamboo.

"You should have stayed back where it's safer," Grant said.

"I came to make sure *you* are safer," Zhong said. "PLA soldiers are quick to shoot."

On the other side of the bamboo, the blood splatter was much more widely distributed, with blotches on branches and tree trunks. Large footprints crushed leaves into the ground. The prints were narrow, with three toes in front and one trailing straight behind. Grant checked the tip of each toe print. A wide claw had punctured the ground another few centimeters.

"I've seen fossilized footprints similar to this my whole career. Predatory dinosaurs. This thing has some seriously dangerous DNA in its family tree."

A trail of broken branches stretched into the forest. Grant followed the path. Ahead, light broke through a hole in the canopy. In the clearing, a gray rock stuck up between stands of bamboo.

The soldier snapped his rifle to his shoulder and aimed at the rock.

"That rock isn't going anywhere," Grant said.

"That is no rock," Zhong said.

Grant looked closer. He could make out one leg, then another. It looked like the animal that attacked them last night. It wasn't moving. A bird landed on top of it and strutted back and forth.

"It looks dead," Grant said.

"Or just sleeping," Zhong replied.

"Thanks for that bit of positivity."

During the next minute or two of observation the animal didn't move. It made no reaction as a second bird joined the first in a promenade along its side. The creature's chest showed no hint of respiration. Self-preservation begged for Grant to head back to the rest of the group before this huge free meal attracted an army of scavengers. But the scientist in him overrode all that common sense.

Grant advanced on the animal with the other two men in tow. The soldier kept his rifle trained on the carcass the whole way in.

The animal was about four meters long and stood at least that high. The beefy body was built for power. The skin was a dark green/dark gray color that blended perfectly into the low light of the forest. If this thing was lying in wait for an ambush, you'd never see it. It had indeed left the footprints Grant had seen. Huge claws protruded from the toes on each foot.

He worked his way around to the front of the creature. The long head with the narrow jaw was very reminiscent of the dragon fossil they'd seen in Mongolia. But while it had the same teeth and the same jaw, it did not have the protruding hollow tusks. It also clearly lacked wings and the spaded tail.

"Do you think this animal could be the source of your people's dragon myths?" he asked.

"It could be," Zhong said. "No one alive has ever actually seen a dragon. And the wisdom skin is always found on partial carcasses washed down from the mountain."

"Someone catches a partial view of a dinosaur, is predisposed to Chinese dragon myths, and I could see a witness swearing they'd seen a dragon. This will not make Laoxin happy."

Along the head and shoulders, bullets had peppered the skin, and with about as much effect as pepper. Most of the bullets still protruded halfway out.

"Tell our benevolent protector I need to borrow his knife," Grant said to Zhong.

Zhong pointed to the large knife on the soldier's belt and said a few words to him. The soldier gave both men a wary look. Zhong said something else in a pleading tone. The soldier slid the knife from its sheath and handed it handle first to Zhong. He never took his eyes or the gun barrel off of Grant. Zhong handed Grant the knife. Grant bent down beside the head.

Grant wedged the knife tip into one of the bullet holes and pried the bullet out. The skin was rock hard and centimeters thick. This stuff made rhino skin look like papyrus. The soldiers' bullets hadn't felled this thing any more than pricks from a rose bush could kill a man. He took a closer look at the head.

The oversized, protruding eyes were closed. The lids looked to have an almost bony texture to them, another excellent protective measure to complement the thick skin. Blood covered the area around one eye. He raised the lid with the knife. The eyeball was missing, the eye socket blasted and gray brain matter splattered inside.

Grant stood up. The nervous soldier tensed and moved his finger to the rifle's trigger. Grant offered the knife back to Zhong, who passed it back to the soldier. The soldier's finger moved back to grip the rifle butt.

"Bullets didn't bring this thing down. The skin is too tough. Strike that, one bullet did. Through the eye socket when the eyelid was open and then it travelled into the braincase. A million-to-one lucky shot."

"One we shouldn't count on making the next time we see one of these. We need to get off this mountain."

"My position before we even started," Grant said.

Zhong explained to the soldier that they were heading back. The soldier looked relieved. The three of them returned to where Mike and Laoxin stood.

"Everything we found," Grant said, "is bad news."

He filled them in on the details about the animal.

"The attacker is not a dragon," Laoxin said.

"Good chance," Mike said, "that the mountain doesn't have dragons."

"There are no wings," Laoxin said in disappointment.

"No wings. Another entirely new species bent on killing us. Wheeee."

"Then we go up to capture dinosaur."

Grant turned to Zhong. "Does 'bent on killing us' not translate into Chinese?"

Laoxin ordered the soldiers up and out. They gathered their gear and prepared to leave. One of them kicked dirt over the dying embers of the fire. Another soldier came up behind the three men and motioned them to start moving. Grant sighed and grabbed his suitcase as Mike shouldered his pack.

Laoxin consulted a map and led the group up the trail Grant had followed. Minutes later, they came to where the dead reptile lay.

"My God, will you look at that," Mike said. "Body like a *barsboldida*, head and claws like a *haplocheius*."

"And some of the features are the same as the dragon fossils. Perhaps they both had a common ancestor. Look at the size of those eyes, though."

"It attacked at night because it can see in the dark," Mike said. "This thing is probably as nocturnal as tarsiers and lemurs."

Laoxin ordered the men to walk by it, kick it to see that it was dead.

"She's telling them to not fear it," Zhong translated. "To see that they can kill them."

"With a lucky shot," Grant said. "I wouldn't count on repelling the next attack, especially by more than one."

The soldiers didn't see it that way. They saw a dead, bloody beast, and smiled and congratulated each other. The group moved into the forest, still following the widened trail the creatures likely made.

Grant wondered how many other lethal species awaited them as they ascended the mountain.

CHAPTER SIXTEEN

An hour later they hadn't encountered any signs of another dinosaur. Grant was not disappointed. The sergeant spoke to Laoxin and she reluctantly called a halt to the group for a break. The panting men dropped in place on the trail. Several broke out cigarettes and began to smoke. Grant sat down on his suitcase.

Laoxin stepped up behind Grant and prodded him in the back with the toe of her boot. "Dinosaur expert. Where we find dinosaur?"

"Ouch! I don't know. It's an unknown species."

"The best place to hunt something," Mike chimed in, "is where it eats or where it drinks. These are carnivores, so that might be the same place. A body of water that attracts prey will attract these predators."

"We follow trail to lake and set ambush," Laoxin said.

"But then what?" Mike said. "You think you can capture one after seeing how bullets barely scratch them?"

"Have tranquilizers. Capture one in nets."

"And drag it down the mountain?"

"We have a plan," Laoxin said, and then walked away.

"I have seen her type all my life," Zhong said. "Self-serving military officers with an agenda. In the end, her plan will only benefit her."

Minutes later, they continued the trek. Laoxin checked her map frequently against a GPS device. As they hiked, they did not find any water sources. Laoxin finally called the group to a halt short of a relatively level location.

She pulled out her satellite phone.

"Look at that," Mike whispered. "That's how we call for help and get the hell out of here."

"I'm sure she'll let us borrow it if we agree to reverse the charge for the call," Grant said. "And who would you call, anyway?"

"I know a guy nearby."

"It's a country with a surging black-market economy. Of course you do."

"Rule #3, buddy. Never go in without a strategy to get out."

The sergeant shouted out a barrage of orders and the soldiers spread out into a circle. They all looked nervous.

A few minutes later, a Chinese fighter-bomber screamed by overhead. A single black bomb hung under one wing.

Laoxin shouted at the soldiers. They hit the ground and crawled for some kind of cover. Grant didn't need Zhong to provide a translation. If the Chinese Army had some beef with the Chinese Air Force, Grant really didn't want anything to do with it. He dove to the ground behind a tree trunk.

The jet banked left, swung around, and headed back, straight for them. The aircraft closed and released its bomb. The plane banked left, kicked in afterburners and climbed. The bomb continued to fly forward and down on what looked like a silent mission to individually annihilate Grant.

But gravity trumped momentum. The bomb dropped faster than it flew forward, and headed for the center of the flat area. Just before impact, it exploded with a blinding flash and a thunderous boom. Shrapnel burst out in all directions. Tree branches, leaves, stalks of bamboo all vaporized into a blizzard of shredded foliage. The concussion blew larger trees over at the roots.

Grant buried his head and closed his eyes as the shock wave approached. It rolled over him like a hurricane and threatened to suck him off the ground. He grabbed an exposed root and held tight. The wind sucked his shirt skyward, but he stayed prone against the mulchy ground. The shock wave passed. He opened his eyes and exhaled.

For once it's a good thing that I haven't lost weight, he thought.

The silence in the aftermath seemed as deafening as the blast itself. Flecks of leaves and bamboo splinters snowed down all around. Grant sat up as Mike and Zhong did the same. Laughter and cheering rose from the soldier's ranks, as if surviving the bomb had been some sort of amusement park ride.

"Everyone okay?" Grant said.

Mike turned to display a shard of bamboo that had impaled his arm. Wet blood soaked his shirt sleeve. "I'll need a little help here," he said through gritted teeth.

"Damn." Grant crawled over.

The shard was two centimeters wide with a bit of a curve to it. The exposed portion was as long as a carving knife. Grant tore away at the hole in Mike's shirt. Blood seeped from around the bamboo.

"No arteries nicked," Grant said. "How deep is it in there?"

"Too damn deep. Hurts like hell. Yank the thing out."

"Seriously?"

"No, I want to walk around like a bamboo pin cushion. Yes, yank it out."

Grant stared at the shard. It even looked like it hurt. He imagined just touching the end of it would send waves of pain through his old friend. He hovered his hand over the giant sliver, first in one position, then another, trying to guess if a certain way to grab it would hurt Mike the least.

"Oh, never mind," Mike said.

He held his breath. In one stroke, he grabbed the shard and pulled. Grant winced. The bamboo slid out of the wound with a slurp. The sharp, bloody tip was several centimeters long. Mike moaned.

"I was about to do that," Grant said.

"Before I bled to death? Thanks for your help. I'll be fine."

"My moral support made the difference, I say."

A green bandage hit the ground beside Grant, followed by an antiseptic wipe in a packet. He looked up to see Tong, the kid with the owlish glasses. He pointed to Mike's bleeding arm and said something.

"He says don't let that get infected," Zhong said.

Grant bowed his head to the boy. The soldier scurried off, as if afraid to get caught by his comrades being compassionate.

Mike tore his shirt sleeve down to the hem. He grabbed the antiseptic packet, ripped it open and swabbed the wound. Blood continued to run from the cut. He bound the wound with the bandage and tied it tight. The bandage stayed dry.

"I'd give push-ups a break if I were you," Grant said.

Mike eased himself upright, favoring his bandaged arm. "Thanks for your medical expertise."

"I *am* a doctor."

As the rest of the soldiers rose and brushed off their gear, Laoxin approached. She gave an order into the satellite phone and then put it back in her pocket.

"What the hell was all that?" Grant said to her. "Does the Chinese Air Force always bomb its army?"

"Not bomb us, bomb forest. Daisy cutter bomb clear a space."

"You know they make chainsaws to do that? There are some guys I met in the Amazon who could—"

The sound of rotor blades cut him off. A large twin-rotor military helicopter flew into view. It carried a big, flat sling load underneath. The chopper hovered to the middle of the blast zone, then lowered the sling load to the ground. The cargo hook released the canvas straps and they snaked down to the earth. The helicopter rose and flew off back down the mountain.

Knowing their next job, the soldiers ran to the sling load. They cut away the strapping and removed huge grids of metal bars. They levered one upright and a soldier pounded metal pegs into the corner with a sledgehammer.

"They're building a cage," Mike said.

"No cage can hold a dragon of Szechuan," Zhong said. "The Scarlet General learned that centuries ago."

The old man had a habit of being right about all things dragon. Grant hoped this would be one of the times he wasn't.

CHAPTER SEVENTEEN

The soldiers around them split into two teams. While some of the group continued to erect the giant cage, the rest set to a different task. Pulling parts from different packs, they began to assemble two long rifles with huge barrels, then they loaded them with tranquilizer darts the size of spray cans.

"That's enough sedative to drop a small town in its tracks," Grant said.

"But is it enough for one dinosaur?" Mike said. "No clue about the weight, the physiology. Too much might kill the dinosaur."

"Too little and the dinosaur kills us."

Laoxin stepped up to the three of them.

"We go hunt dinosaur," Laoxin said. "Find lake for ambush."

"That's the royal 'we' in use there, right?" Grant said.

Laoxin just stared at him. "We go hunt dinosaur. Back before dark. One dinosaur expert only. One stay here to fill the cage."

"I'll go this time," Mike said.

"With that arm wound?" Grant said. "No way."

Laoxin stepped away to round up the hunting team. Mike leaned over to Grant.

"Get that satellite phone," he whispered. "My China contacts can help get us out of here."

Zhong went to one of the soldiers assembling the tranq guns. He motioned to the empty backpack at his feet and said a few sentences. The soldier nodded. Zhong retrieved the pack and brought it to Grant.

"Better than a suitcase," he said.

Grant wanted to kiss the man. "Thank you so much."

Grant shoved the contents of his bag into the pack. Then Grant and Zhong joined the hunting team. Ten soldiers including two of them armed with the tranquilizer rifles. They looked eager for the hunt.

"Do these guys have some kind of death wish?" Grant said.

"From what I overhear," Zhong said, "they have been promised a cut of the profits from the PLA. They all plan on being rich."

"If I wasn't about to be killed by a dinosaur, I'd note the irony of Communist soldiers working with capitalistic motivation."

"It is a new China," Zhong said.

The soldiers began to trek single-file uphill along one of the animal trails. A rifleman led the way, followed by Grant and Zhong. The tranq men hung further back with Laoxin. Apparently, she wanted close control over that limited resource.

The steep mountain slope made the going slow for the heavily-laden soldiers, but even that reduced pace put a strain on Grant. Despite the cooler temperature, sweat soon soaked his shirt. Zhong seemed unaffected and the thin old man ascended without effort. Grant wondered if there was something to all those herbal medicines Zhong sold in his store.

The smell of asphalt soon filled the air. The incongruity of something so industrialized in a place so primeval made Grant pause. It also made him think about hamburger stands beside highways on hot summer days, which didn't make the granola bars in his backpack any more appetizing.

A few minutes later, the soldier at the head of the patrol stopped. He shouted something back to the group.

"He says 'black river'," Zhong translated.

Grant moved forward to where the soldier stood. The asphalt smell ramped up to choking level. In front of them ran a creek of rushing tar.

"How could someone dump this here?" Zhong said.

"No, this is runoff from a natural seep. Oil trapped between layers of canted rock runs sideways and up to the surface. This isn't common here?"

"I have never seen anything like this."

"The smell and the danger of seeps like this might have contributed to people placing the mountain off-limits generations ago. We do not want to step in that. Tell the soldier to follow it uphill on this side of the stream."

Zhong relayed the order. The soldier looked relieved to comply and the group continued up with the stream on the right.

Further up, the tar stream curved across their path. A fallen, narrow tree lay across the stream. If they wanted to keep heading uphill, this would be the place to cross. The soldier stopped and asked a question of Zhong.

"He wants to know if he should cross the stream."

"If he can."

The tree wasn't much wider than the soldier's boots. The soldier gave it a kick. It rocked a bit but seemed relatively stable. He climbed on top of it, caught his balance, and then practically ran across it. He hopped off on the other side and shouted something back to Zhong as he laughed.

"No one likes a show-off," Grant said.

"He says it is like the obstacle course in training."

"Believe it or not, I missed PLA basic training."

Zhong followed the soldier across. The nimble old man practically danced across the log. Grant contemplated hating him for it.

By now, the rest of the expedition had caught up, and Grant was the obvious roadblock. Using some whimsical physics, he hoped that the weight of his stomach and the extra weight of the pack on his back would balance and make him more stable. He stepped up on the end of the tree trunk and immediately found that theory to be untrue. He wobbled back and forth until finally having to step off the log.

"You swim the stream instead, maybe?" Laoxin said as she laughed.

Grant was afraid he'd cross the log *and* swim the creek at this rate. And no one swam a tar river. He'd just sink in it.

Grant stepped back up on the log. The stream was only five or six meters wide, but from on top of the log it seemed like kilometers. And the current promised that the creek was deep. He held out both arms for balance. It didn't seem to help but it did make him wish he could flap them and fly over the creek.

Step by step he edged out across the creek. From right over the oily flow, the smell became near unbearable, like being submerged in a tub of used motor oil laced with sulphur. Every imperfection in the tree bark seemed determined to send the sole of his shoe sliding sideways.

Seconds seemed like hours. He checked his progress. Less than halfway across.

"Faster!" Laoxin shouted at him.

He wanted to shout something rude back at her, but didn't think he could counterbalance the force of the air he would expel from his lungs as he yelled. He kept moving forward, sliding one foot after the other across the tree trunk.

With a meter left to go, the idea that he might touch earth again began to be credible. He smiled.

"I'm going to make it," he said to himself.

He took a bolder step.

Both his feet shot out from beneath him. He dropped straight down, landing straddling the tree trunk, and compressing the family jewels. The pain between his legs shot straight up his spine. But all he could think about was not drowning in the torrent of tar rushing beneath him. Despite the pain, he wrapped both arms around the trunk and clung on.

"Go faster," Laoxin yelled again.

Grant moaned. No way he could stand back up without teetering into the creek. He pulled himself forward with his arms until he got close to the other side. Then Zhong and the lead soldier each grabbed one of his arms and pulled him the last half-meter. He rolled off the log and onto his back on the ground. Zhong's face loomed over him.

"Are you okay?"

"Just great," he wheezed. "I wasn't planning on having children anyway. And I couldn't pass up a moment of indignity like this."

The rest of the soldiers crossed over the tree trunk without incident. Grant got to his feet as Laoxin jumped off the tree.

"You waste time," she said. "Find dragon now."

Grant hobbled up to where Zhong waited.

"Does it hurt?" Zhong said.

"Only when I move my legs. Let's go. Have the soldier keep following the River Styx here."

The group set out again and Grant walked off the pain in his groin. After following the stinking stream for a while, an animal's roar came from up ahead. The leaves around them shook. Grant recognized it as the same roar that had swept through camp the night of the attack. The group dropped to a knee as if on command. Grant's heart threatened to beat right out of his chest.

The lead soldier looked back and said something.

"A trapped dinosaur," Zhong translated.

Grant's ears perked up. He peered through the leaves but saw nothing.

"My sense of self-preservation says run," Grant said. "But emboldened by the safety implied by the word 'trapped', the quest for knowledge says we go check this out."

"The quest for knowledge gets people killed."

"Hopefully not today."

They advanced in a crouch to where the soldier sat. On the other side of the trees, a lake of oozing pitch, the source of the stream they followed, covered several hectares. Near the far side, one of the creatures that attacked the camp stood half submerged in the ooze. The freshly turned ground behind it hadn't supported its weight and the collapse had sent the creature into the sticky lake. It raised its head to the sky and cried out a plaintive, high pitched scream.

Grant was reminded of the La Brea tar pit in Los Angeles, where thousands of bones from extinct animals had been unearthed. This was a replay of what had happened there, thousands of years ago. The thing in the lake would have killed Grant without thinking, but he could not help but feel some compassion for the helpless creature.

Laoxin came up behind them with one of the tranq-wielding soldiers. "What is this?"

"One of the dinosaurs like the ones that attacked us is trapped in the lake," Grant said.

"We kill it before it escapes."

"It's not escaping. Nothing gets out of a pitch lake."

The animal cried out again, begging for salvation, or perhaps a speedier death.

A response echoed across the sky. Unlike the bellowing roar of the trapped animal, this cry was a high-pitched shriek that sent a shiver up Grant's spine. A sound like the flapping of a great circus tent came from overhead.

Then it flew into view, an enormous dragon, three times the size of the fossil in the desert. Grant's jaw dropped open. There actually were dragons.

Its wings spanned almost ten meters and a whip-like spaded tail snaked out half again as long. White, sharp teeth jutted from its long, menacing jaw. Red irises flashed in its eyes. The creature in the lake was scary. This dragon was terrifying.

Grant looked over at Zhong. The old man stared transfixed at the creature. He mumbled some Chinese that sounded reverential.

"I'm going to reassess my theory that there are no dragons on the mountain," Grant said.

The dragon angled for the dinosaur in the tar. Apparently, the dragon had discovered a meal ripe for the picking.

The reptile in the ooze roared. The dragon's wings swept back and it flared as it approached the creature. The claws at the tips of all four feet spread out to crush the prey beneath it.

The dragon hit its target. Its feet clamped on the dinosaur. But its jaws did not snap around and crush the reptile's neck. The dragon's feet did not shred the helpless animal's hide. Instead, with several mighty flaps of its wings, the dragon began to extract the animal from the tar. With each flap the powerful muscles along the dragon's legs bulged and the animal in its grasp rose another meter out of the muck. Finally, the dinosaur broke free with a slurp of resistant tar. All four legs flailed in the air, sending thick, black splatters back onto the surface of the lake. The dragon set it down on the shore. Then it alighted beside it, bent its head and appeared to drink from the oily liquid.

Laoxin slapped the tranq-gunner on the back of the helmet. She barked an order and pointed at the dragon. The gunner shook himself out of an awe-struck stupor and aimed at the dragon. He fired and the gun coughed out a dart. But the weapon's range was far too short, and the dart dropped point-first into the lake.

The dragon raised its head and narrowed its eyes at the spot where the dart had splashed down. Then it took to the air and flew up the mountain.

The dinosaur beside the lake tried in vain to shake the tar from its skin, then moved off to the right around the lake's far side.

Laoxin smacked the gunner again, and growled an admonishment, as if the laws of physics were somehow his fault. She pointed left and said something in Chinese.

"She says follow the dragon," Zhong sighed.

"The dragon? If we have to try and capture something, let's stick to the dinosaur. At least it doesn't fly."

"You are not Chinese. You do not understand. The dragon is too symbolic to pass up. And that is what she promised her superiors."

The soldiers rose and began to move along the lake shore. Grant and Zhong went with them.

"The dinosaur was easy prey," Zhong said. "Why didn't the dragon kill it?"

"It wasn't because dragons are vegetarians," Grant said. "But the dragon didn't just fly by and skip an easy meal. It went out of its way to save it, drawn by the cry of distress. Your stories don't paint the dragons as particularly altruistic."

"They are blood-thirsty killers."

"Then the dinosaurs are worth something to the dragon. And interspecies interdependence is rare."

Zhong gave him a look of incomprehension. Grant realized that few of the words in his last sentence were likely part of any English language class.

"Different animals rarely work together," he said.

The stench of the tar receded as they moved away from the lake. But the further forward they pushed, the deeper the pit in Grant's stomach grew. The dinosaurs were big. The dragon was huge. Having two apex predators at the top of the local food chain made his odds of survival even slimmer. He had no confidence that either long range bullets or short-range darts would be enough to keep this group alive. This time Grant's sense of self-preservation came out on top. Following that dragon was a very bad idea.

CHAPTER EIGHTEEN

The sun was well past its zenith, and the soldiers hadn't taken a break since lunch, hours ago. Grant was no orienteering expert, in fact would probably even misspell it, but they'd traveled so long that it didn't seem like Laoxin was going to hold to her "back before dark" promise. Since they'd sighted the dragon, she had driven the soldiers hard as they scaled the steepening side of the mountain.

The trail broke out of the woods to reveal a stone wall many meters high, blackened by mildew. Bamboo grew around the edge and sprouted on top between the castellated battlements. The group stopped and stared.

"Ah," Zhong exhaled in wonder. "The lost palace of the Scarlet General."

"Who?"

"The warlord who tried to claim the mountain and subjugate the dragons."

Grant thought back to his expedition into the Amazon. "In my experience, no good ever comes of rediscovering lost royal structures."

The group skirted the edge of the wall until they came upon a doorway. Two great metal doors hung open and askew. The soldiers pushed them aside with great effort and the group entered.

From the inside, the size of the palace was more apparent. The walls bounded an interior courtyard that was about fifty meters long on each side. A single-story building in the center looked to be about fifteen hundred square meters with a classic Chinese pillared design. Only the edges of the concave roof remained and black mold and green fungus obscured most of the building's red paint. Zhong gave the collapsing building a reverential, awestruck look.

"Doesn't look like the Scarlet General won the dragon battle," Grant said.

"Legend says his first-born son broke the taboo," Zhong said, "and went hunting on the mountain. He vanished and days later a dragon dropped his charred corpse at the valley palace of the Scarlet General."

"Because the dragon would have the general's home address?" Grant said.

Zhong continued without acknowledgement. "Enraged at the loss of his son, he vowed to kill all dragons. The Scarlet General forced a thousand men up the mountain to build these walls. When dragons slew that thousand, he forced up a thousand more. The dragon attacks relented, and the Scarlet General sensed victory was near. The walls were completed and he marched his entire army into the palace, and prepared them to move out and destroy the dragons in their lairs.

"But it had all been a trap set by the dragons. Once the soldiers were in the palace, the dragons lay siege, and cut off all resupply from the mountain's base. In weeks, the men were starving. Then the dragons attacked. The dragons slaughtered them all, save for one soldier allowed to escape, to tell the story of the dragons roasting the Scarlet General alive by the fire they breathed, and to warn the world to leave the mountain to them."

Grant thought that embellished myth was likely only half true, but half true was still all bad news when you stood in the ruins of the palace of the Scarlet General. The building in the courtyard center didn't destroy itself.

But his current worry was keeping dinosaurs from eating him. The perimeter walls were high enough to keep at least the dinosaurs at bay, and that made camping here certainly better than a night in the forest. The soldiers seemed to have thought the same thing as two of them were busy aligning the metal doors in the wall and setting a metal cross-member in place behind them.

Hope swelled in Grant that Professor Carson had discovered this palace when he'd explored the mountain. Certainly, if he'd come across the walls he could not have passed it by without investigating. The old man could have slid between the opening in those big metal doors. Even if he'd just spent the night, he might have left some trace.

Zhong climbed the steps to the ruined building, then stepped inside in an awed trance. Grant followed him in. The empty interior was a mess, with a thick layer of dirt and leaves covering the floor. The center had originally hosted a raised dais, but it appeared to have been blasted away, with three charred columns at the corners and the remains of the dais collapsed into a hole at the center.

"From here, the Scarlet General would command his army," Zhong said, "with officers in armor awaiting his orders."

Zhong bent down and swept away the dirt in front of the dais with his hands. He exposed a tile floor inlaid with a beautiful mosaic of a dragon in flight. Flames flickered from its mouth. Archers had just loosed a volley and the burning arrows promised to seal the dragon's fate. Having seen the thick skin on the dinosaurs, Grant thought this depiction of victorious combat a little fanciful. Those arrows probably wouldn't even break the creature's skin.

Grant walked up the dais steps. A jagged-edged hole consumed the dais center. Grant leaned in and looked down into darkness. Earthy, humid air rose up against his face. Even with the roof open to the sky, Grant couldn't make out a thing. He shined a flashlight into the opening, but the darkness consumed the beam and it revealed nothing. If Carson had fallen down into that abyss, no way he'd survived.

"Definitely skipping the tour of the basement," Grant said.

He returned to Zhong, who was still staring at the dragon mosaic.

"This is amazing," Zhong said. "To have the stories of your ancestors be proven true."

"I'd like it better if your stories had happy endings," Grant said.

CHAPTER NINETEEN

As night fell, Mike felt more anxious about being alone at the cage site with the soldiers.

With their leader Laoxin gone, the sergeant seemed only nominally in charge. That left personal greed as the troops' prime motivator. And while he appreciated the way greed could focus someone on an objective, that focus was often at the expense of all other things, and he was afraid he was in the "all other things" category to these soldiers.

He leaned against a tree at the clearing's edge and winced at the pain in his injured arm. The bamboo shard had done more damage than he'd let on. The wound felt hot, and hot meant infection, and infection meant trouble. Who knew what kind of nasty crap that bamboo had picked up and then injected into his body? He needed to get out of here before his medical condition got out of hand.

He also wanted to get out turning a profit. He hadn't lied to Grant about signing up for this expedition because he'd wanted to find Professor Carson. But you can't teach an old dog a new moral code, and seeing that dragon fossil in the desert had made his mouth water. That piece was good for a bucketful of cash to a museum, three bucketsful to a private collector. And in a country so rife with endemic corruption, he knew he could find a way to spirit the thing out of the People's Republic of Repression. For now, he'd keep that on the back burner, a problem to solve when he was back in the USA to make a plan. But he was sure as hell going to keep his eyes open for anything else that might help defray some of this trip's expenses.

And while Grant still had faith the professor would wander out of the forest alive, Mike didn't. When Zhong told them Carson had disappeared weeks ago, Mike held out little hope. After the dinosaur attack, he had none. If this group he was with barely survived an attack, an individual had no chance at all.

Shadows grew long and the men hammered the final side of the cage together. It stood tall and narrow, four meters on one side but almost three times as long and the same measurement high. Mike went to give the cage a closer inspection. The bars appeared to be stainless steel, each a few centimeters thick. The cage was big enough to hold the dinosaur they'd encountered last night. He wondered if it was strong enough to keep it inside.

The soldiers then began to collect piles of branches shattered by the bombing. In short order they had four piles, each spaced evenly away from a corner of the cage. The kindling was lit and soon four bonfires marked the cage's perimeter. The pyres put the cage area in near daylight. The soldiers kept a minimal watch on the blast zone perimeter, apparently hoping the fires would keep any creatures at bay.

But while that might be good conventional wisdom, the idea hadn't worked last night. The dinosaur hadn't been frightened by the fire at all, had no issue with charging it and the men around it. These soldiers were making a mistake.

Mike approached the sergeant as he stoked a fire. He hoped he could talk some sense into the man with his rudimentary Chinese.

"The fires are a bad idea," he said in Chinese. He waved his hands in the air. "Too big. Too bright."

The sergeant shoved him away with a look of contempt on his face. Mike had a feeling that even if the man spoke perfect English, he'd have gotten the same response. He stepped away and picked his pack up off the ground. Laoxin might have had him stay back to share his dinosaur expertise, but that didn't mean these idiots were going to listen to him.

He walked to the far side of the cage and decided to find a place to sleep that night. The bomb had blown most of the vegetation flat, but there wasn't much open, level space to bed down. He'd need to clear himself a spot somewhere.

Tong, the young soldier with the owlish glasses approached him. He looked scared.

"Hello, Mike."

"Hey, Tong. Any chance you have a way to get us the hell out of here?"

Tong didn't look like he understood. Mike assumed he wouldn't.

"Very scary," Tong said.

"Yes, very scary."

Tong pulled his canteen from his hip and offered it to Mike. Mike took a deep drink of water. He hadn't realized how dehydrated he was. He wiped his mouth and handed the canteen back to Tong.

"Thanks, kid."

Tong responded with a shallow bow and returned to the rest of the soldiers.

Mike went back to his search for a place to lie down. He found a dry, level spot and began to pull away fallen branches and sweep away the earth.

From the dark of the forest came a dinosaur's roar.

The soldiers froze in place. They shouted warnings. Rifles clicked as rounds were chambered. Mike jumped to his feet.

From over the bonfire to his left appeared the head of a dinosaur. It held a dead deer in its mouth. It cocked its head at the sight of the cage, then dropped the deer to one side. Its mouth opened wide and the flames reflected off a row of sharp teeth. It roared and the sound rattled the open door of the steel cage. The creature certainly wasn't afraid of the fire.

Like a delayed echo, dinosaur roars sounded from the other three corners of the clearing. With the crush of branches and the tromp of heavy footfalls, a dinosaur loomed out of the darkness beside each bonfire. One of them carried a squirming sun bear in its mouth. It saw the cage and dropped the bear. The animal scampered away into the shadows.

The soldiers ran for the cage door.

That seemed like a good plan. Strong enough to keep a dino in had to be strong enough to keep a dino out. Mike grabbed his pack and made a run for the door.

Two steps in, his foot caught on a felled branch. The added weight of his pack drove him down hard. He cracked his head against a tree trunk and the world made a looping spin before his eyes. He pulled himself up and staggered to the cage door.

Just as he reached it, a panicked soldier slammed it shut and locked a chain around the bars.

"What the hell?" Mike yelled.

From all four corners, the dinosaurs charged. A fusillade of rifle fire erupted from inside the cage in all directions. Bullets whizzed by and Mike dropped to his knees in front of the door. He checked behind him.

The earth rumbled as the four furious dinosaurs charged the cage. Bullets were not stopping them.

CHAPTER TWENTY

Staying pinned against the cage was suicide. But making a run for it wasn't much better.

However, with two dinosaurs bearing down on his side of the cage, Mike reacted with panic-driven instinct and ran. Blood thundered in his ears as his heart jumped into an adrenaline-fueled overdrive that temporarily masked the pain in his arm and his sketchy equilibrium. He looked straight ahead and recalled running a football play in high school against a surging defensive line. He prayed that the dinosaurs on each side would be so focused on the cage that they would miss his escape.

His prayer went unanswered.

The dinosaur to his left altered his course to intercept. Mike pumped his legs faster. The dinosaur lunged. At the last second, Mike ducked and the dinosaur's jaws clamped on Mike's pack. It lifted him off the ground and he hung in the air by the straps. In his mind, he saw the creature tossing him straight up, then biting him in two on the way down. He closed his eyes and said goodbye to the world.

But the dino seemed to have the cage as its ultimate prize. It swung its head and sent Mike sailing past one of the bonfires. He hit the ground backpack first and skidded into a fallen tree.

He opened his eyes to a view of the cage besieged by four dinosaurs. They tried to bite at the bars but the rods were too close together. The gunfire from the soldiers seemed to only further enrage the animals as bullets bit into their thick skin. In frustrated fury, the dinosaurs slammed their bodies against the cage. Two of them hit it in unison. The cage rocked up on one side, then dropped back down to the ground.

The soldiers got off a few more shots. The firing stopped and soldiers slapped pockets and ammo pouches in a vain search for more ammunition. The shouting between them contained a hint of panic.

Two dinosaurs lined up on one side of the cage. In unison, they swung their bodies against the bars. The cage teetered and then fell over on its long side. The soldiers tumbled to the down side. A man's bone snapped followed by a shriek of pain.

The four dinosaurs roared in response. They surrounded the cage, rose up on their hind legs and dropped down front legs first on the cage. The steel moaned under the weight. Back and forth, the dinosaurs rose and dropped onto the cage. With each plunge the bars deformed a bit more and the cage flattened into a smaller living space.

Inside, the soldiers screamed as they hugged the ground to avoid the collapsing steel bars. One tried to wedge his rifle between the walls as a brace. Dinosaur legs dropped beside it and shattered the rifle. Meter by meter the cage compressed until it touched the soldier's backs. Their screams for salvation made Mike wince.

All the dinosaurs backed away, then one charged. At the last second it jumped surprisingly high and far, and landed square on the center of the cage. Soldiers hollered out one final blood-curdling chorus. Then the forest went silent save for the crackle of the four bonfires.

The four dinosaurs went to opposite corners of the mangled cage and began to pry up damaged bars one at a time. One dinosaur's head darted down into an opening and extracted a screaming soldier. Its jaws clamped shut and snapped him in half.

The soldiers were all as good as dead. He wasn't going to hang around and join them. Time to make a break for it while the dinosaurs were distracted.

Downhill made sense. Getting out of the Forest of Fire would be a nice idea. But there were soldiers at the village who would wonder why he came back alone and assume he'd killed the others. And it was a full day's trek back down in the dark, all the while nursing his injured arm.

Hiking uphill, toward where the dragons lived, was suicidal on the face of it. But the other team was much closer than the village, and the tranq guns might keep huge creatures at bay. Signs along the trail they'd used through the forest were fresh enough he could follow it with his flashlight.

Hell of a situation when hiking towards dragons is the best option, he thought.

Now that the adrenaline had abated, all the pain in his arm rolled back in full force. He stood, tightened the straps on his pack and picked his way through the blast debris to the edge of the clear cut. The light from the fires grew dimmer and he flicked on a flashlight. Behind him metal bars screeched and a soldier whimpered in terror.

He found the trail and began to hike uphill.

CHAPTER TWENTY-ONE

Mike made his way upslope with great difficulty. His arm felt like it was on fire and babying it made him shift the weight of his pack so far to one side that his back was starting to feel strained. But after hauling his gear this far, he wasn't going to abandon it now.

As he walked, he played the flashlight beam across the trail the soldiers had broken through the forest. They hadn't tried being stealthy. Snapped branches lined the trail. Discarded food wrappers littered the ground. Dinosaurs could take their pick of sight or smell to hunt down this group if they wanted to.

Mike preferred he got to them first.

An unnatural smell soon permeated the forest, something industrial, kind of petrochemical. Maybe there had been a plane crash up here and he was going to come upon the wreckage.

He discovered the smell's source just before he stepped into it. A black, oily creek cut through the forest. He'd seen where natural oil seeps had contaminated rivers, but never this heavily. If this stuff could be refined, this mountain would be worth a fortune. Except for the dinosaurs killing all the oil roughnecks, of course. Not that the Chinese sweated a little loss of human life in the quest for cash.

He kept the stream to his right and followed the trail upstream. He came across a narrow tree trunk that spanned the stream. The muddy prints along the top testified that the soldiers had used it to cross the stream.

But they'd done it in daylight.

He wondered how Grant had managed it being so out of shape. Perhaps he hadn't.

He gave the trunk a kick. It seemed solid. He stood on top of it. Crossing it wouldn't be easy with the added weight of his pack. He slipped it off and judged the distance across the creek. Could he toss it to the other side? If it fell short into the rushing ooze, he'd lose the gear inside that might get him the hell out of here. Of course, if he drowned in a slurry of petrochemical sludge wearing his pack, having his gear with him would be a moot point.

He grabbed the pack by the handles and, like a shot putter, made a few circles to gain some momentum. His wounded arm screamed about the exertion. One more turn and then he let the bag fly.

It sailed over the creek and hit the ground with a thud.

"One down, me to go," he said to himself.

He could do it quickly or he could do it slowly. His usual rationale was that doing anything slowly just meant more time to screw up. He opted for that way of looking at this. Without the weight of his pack, he felt pretty agile.

He stood on the end of the log, took a deep breath, and went for it.

He crossed the log at a brisk pace, and momentum helped him keep his balance. In several strides he was almost across. He jumped the last step and landed beside the trunk. His foot kicked free one of the rocks that helped hold it in place. He felt lucky that one of the soldiers hadn't done that before he'd made his crossing.

"Hey, Mike!" whispered a voice from the other side of the creek.

Mike turned and shined his flashlight across the fallen tree. On the other side of the creek stood Tong. His uniform was torn and he looked like he'd been through hell. Mike couldn't believe he'd made it out of the cage.

"Tong?"

"Safe now." He sighed with relief. "Go with you to my brother."

A dozen immigration laws and Mike's personal preference was going to keep that from happening.

"Hey, kid. You need—"

Trees rustled somewhere behind Tong. He turned and looked into the darkness. When he turned back around his face was white.

"Mike?" Tong said.

More trees rustled. Louder. Closer. A large branch snapped.

Mike raised his flashlight beam up above Tong's head.

It lit up the head of a dinosaur, just meters behind the boy. The creature blinked against the flashlight beam.

"Kid," Mike said in a low voice, "don't move."

Tong shivered in fear. Mike thought Tong might be able to outrun the dinosaur if he sprinted across the log.

Then Mike wondered if the dinosaur could jump the stream and get to his side. He'd seen one jump higher and further to crush the cage to the ground. He sure didn't want to find out first-hand if this dinosaur had the same skill.

He'd have to give the dinosaur a reason to stay on that side of the creek.

He held up a hand to signal Tong to stay still. The boy nodded rapid fire.

Then Mike kicked the loose end of the tree trunk down into the oily creek. The current caught it and pulled the log downstream.

"Sorry, kid."

Tong screamed. The dinosaur pounced on him and drove him to the ground. Mike turned away and shouldered his pack. He found the trail again with his flashlight beam, and headed uphill.

Behind him, Tong's next scream was cut short, then followed by the sound of tearing flesh. Mike quickened his pace. No need to tempt the dinosaur to the other side of the creek after its snack.

CHAPTER TWENTY-TWO

Zhong and Grant had eaten dinner in the dark on the steps of the collapsed building. Night's arrival had kept them from investigating much more of the palace grounds. They walked over to double-check the security of the main gates. The metal cross beam holding them in place seemed unbreakable.

"Physiologically, these dinosaurs weren't built to be climbers," Grant said. "Their legs aren't powerful enough to pull their weight straight up." He gave the stone wall a slap. "And they are not going to knock this wall down."

"But dragons could still fly over," Zhong said.

"I'm going to start calling you Mr. Silver Lining," Grant said.

Grant couldn't deny that Zhong was right. The dragons *could* fly over. Laoxin had placed tranq-gunners on the top of the wall, but who's to say that the dragons could not glide in silently in the darkness and pluck the soldiers off the battlement, or that the gunners could even hit their targets in the dark.

Now I'm Mr. Silver Lining, Grant thought.

Zhong rubbed his hand against the wall beside the main gate. Moss flaked away and he uncovered part of a carved inscription. He scrounged a stick from the ground and scraped away a larger section. The inscription was uneven and appeared carved in haste.

"Here the Scarlet General made his final stand," Zhong read. "Fear all dragons."

"That's not encouraging," Grant said. "And the Scarlet General had an entire army to back him up."

The corners of the enclosure each had a small tower with narrow firing slits and a single door that opened to the top of the wall. Grant and Zhong went to the base of one tower and ascended the circular stone staircase within. When they got to the top, it took both of them to break the rusty hinges free and shove the door open.

The wall rose just above the tops of the trees and gave an unimpeded view of the night sky. A breeze from the east cleared most of the pollution and the silver stars seemed infinite against the black sky. Other mountains to the west blocked a view of inland China, but even this far away, the glow of Chengdu lighted the night. The village of Zhōng Xiū far away at the mountain's base lay dark. Zhong looked in that direction and his shoulders sagged.

"I'm sure everyone there is okay," Grant said.

"Lights are few there. But the village is dark every night. Tradition says that the dragons are attracted to light at night."

"Well, the dinosaurs certainly were to the campfire."

"I am sad for more than just my people. If Laoxin does not bring back a dragon, the PLA will wipe this mountain clean of my village."

"They could just send a larger force in."

"You do not understand the Chinese way. The dragon symbolizes power and wisdom to our people, from a time long before Communist rule. A dragon defeating the army would be an ill omen to the ruling class, and an inspiration to those who feel oppressed. The government could not lose face failing in battle here. Sending in a second, larger force would admit the failure of the first. The government way is to suppress and erase. If Laoxin fails, the next bombs that drop will not just flatten a few trees."

"They would destroy your village rather than risk word of failure getting out to the rest of the country?"

"In an instant."

"Then we should help capture the dragon. Then they will let your people live?"

"My people, yes. But you? Do you think they want to admit they needed the help of two Americans to subdue a dragon?"

"Zhong, as a motivational speaker, you need some work."

Down below, something crashed through branches. The soldier along the wall shouted a warning and trained his pistol at the tree line. Grant's pulse quickened. He stepped next to the soldier and peered down over the wall. The soldier turned on a flashlight and played the beam across the forest.

A few branches swayed as the light crossed the trees. The beam backed up and spotlighted the shaking leaves. The soldier aimed his pistol along the beam.

Suddenly Mike staggered out of the foliage, eyes wide, shirt soaked in sweat, backpack torn and askew. The soldier moved his finger to the trigger.

Grant lunged at the pistol. "Don't shoot!" He pressed the barrel down against the top of the wall. The soldier hurled a curse Grant's way.

Mike looked up in confusion from the base of the wall. "Grant? Let me in!"

Behind Mike, a tree shuddered then fell sideways. Mike lurched out of its path and hit the ground.

A dinosaur charged into the beam of the soldier's flashlight. It roared and sent the hairs on Grant's neck to attention. He yanked the soldier's pistol up off the wall.

"Shoot! Shoot! What are you waiting for?"

The dinosaur spotted Mike and turned toward him to attack. The soldier opened fire with the pistol. Rounds hit the dinosaur's head and with a roar, it turned its attention to the soldier. The creature lunged at the wall. It went up on its hind legs, but its head was still well below the battlement. The soldier fired two rounds down its throat. Other soldiers along the wall rushed to his aid.

With the dinosaur distracted, Grant saw his chance to get Mike in through the gate. He ran past Zhong for the stairway down. He entered the small building and bounded down the slick, uneven steps.

Two soldiers appeared at the base of the stairs, rifles at the ready. They charged up the stairs two abreast. Grant was halfway down. They were not leaving him any room. One of them shouted for him to get out of the way. As if there was somewhere for him to go.

The soldier's closed on him without slowing. They were going to knock him off the stairway on the open side. He looked over the edge. A long drop to a stone floor. A premonition of having two broken ankles appeared. But if he didn't jump, he'd surely be pushed.

"How does this stuff keep happening to me?" he said.

He jumped.

The ground came up faster than he expected. He held his breath and landed on his toes. His back compressed like a spring and he ended up in a squat. But somehow he stayed upright and managed not to snap any bones. He stood up, a bit stunned by his luck.

"That wasn't so bad," he said.

Above, one of the ascending soldiers dislodged a bit of stone off the staircase. It plummeted down and hit Grant on the head. Grant cursed and headed for the main gate.

Gunfire sounded from the wall above him. The deeper bangs of rifles joined the sharper crack of the pistol. The dinosaur roared and the creature threw itself against the other side of the wall. Rock chips flurried down but the wall held. Grant ran to the doors and raised the crossbeam. He opened it. Mike pushed through from the other side and collapsed on the ground. Grant slammed the door shut behind him and dropped the crossbeam bar back in place.

More gunfire came from above them. The dinosaur roared in frustration and the wall took another pounding. Laoxin ran up, pistol drawn. She aimed it at Mike, then relaxed after recognizing him. Grant knelt beside Mike.

"What happened?"

"Dinosaurs overran us. Crushed the cage. I barely escaped."

"The rest of the soldiers?" Laoxin said.

"All dead."

Grant recalculated their survival odds with under half the soldiers. The number came up close to zero.

Laoxin cursed and then rushed up the stairs to the top of the wall. Grant pulled Mike to his feet and they followed her up.

By now all the soldiers had arrayed themselves along the battlement. They kept up a steady fire, striking the dinosaur along its spine and flanks. The dinosaur seemed more annoyed than injured. One of the tranq-gunners aimed his rifle at the beast.

"No," shouted Laoxin.

She pressed the rifle barrel away from the dinosaur. She added something in Chinese.

From up the mountain, the high-pitched scream of a dragon rolled across the treetops. Then a ball of flame lit a distant spot above the tree line. The dinosaur swiveled its head in that direction and raised its nose in the air. It dropped down and re-entered the forest in the fireball's direction.

"She told the soldier to save the dart for the dragons," Zhong said.

"Dragons?" Mike said.

"We saw one on the way here," Grant said. He stepped up next to Laoxin. "Are you nuts? Half your men are dead, the cage destroyed, and you still want to hunt a dragon?"

"No mission too difficult for the People's Liberation Army. A helicopter pick up cage with sleeping dragon in it. Instead, helicopter pick up sleeping dragon without cage. You help or you get to sit outside wall."

"If we are checking for druthers," Grant said, "I'm an 'inside the wall' kind of guy."

Laoxin turned and barked orders at the soldiers. They dispersed along the wall.

"She cannot return without the dragon," Zhong said. "The PLA will execute her."

"So she'll keep up the hunt," Mike said. "Even if it kills all of us."

CHAPTER TWENTY-THREE

The short remainder of the night passed quietly with no further dinosaur attacks. The rising sun awakened Grant from the world's most uncomfortable sleep on the steps of the ruined palace building. A heavy dew soaked him to the skin and visions of dying of hypothermia made an unwelcome arrival. He strapped his glasses back on his head.

Mike had already started a small fire at the building's far end. He and Zhong sat near it. Grant's whole body seemed to creak as he stood up. He limped over and joined them.

"Rise and shine," Mike said.

"Another day in paradise," Grant said. "What time does the breakfast buffet open?"

He stood over the fire and let the rising heat warm his face. His shirt began to steam.

"What did the soldiers at the cage do to provoke a dinosaur attack?" he asked.

"They set fires around the cage, thinking they would keep the creatures at bay. But each fire seemed to attract a dinosaur instead. The dinosaurs stood right next to the bonfires."

"Odd. Animals for the most part have a hard-wired fear of fire."

"Not these things. They even paused their dinners to investigate. Two had captured prey in their jaws when they arrived."

"Prey?"

"A deer and a bear."

"That's bizarre. That would be like a lion catching a hyrax and carrying it around instead of devouring it. Smaller creatures are snacks, the equivalent of us impulse purchasing a candy bar in the check-out line."

"Whatever they had, they dropped it as soon as they saw the human prey. You should have seen them crush that steel cage like matchsticks."

"Which leads me to believe that it would not have held a dragon once it came out of its dart-induced coma. And Laoxin thinks that she's going to tie one up and have a helicopter fly it out of here? I can't even get a cat to the vet without the thing wounding me."

Grant searched through his pack and found his last crushed granola bar in the bottom. He extracted it. It had the structure of a bag of sand. Once this was gone, he was going to spend this trip hungry. Despite being Communists, he didn't think that the soldiers would be putting all the food in a community pot for equal distribution to all.

"How's the arm?" Grant asked Mike.

"Hurts and hot. Not a good combo."

"We need to find a way out of here before we die of some combination of starvation, infection, dinosaur teeth, and bullets," Grant said.

He poured his granola gravel into his mouth. He pretended it was Belgian waffles. That didn't help.

"There's one door to get through the palace wall," Mike said. "And those soldiers won't let us take it."

"Maybe there's another door, or a hole in the wall. Now that it's light out, I'll go check."

"Knock yourself out," Mike said.

The fire hadn't dried Grant's shirt completely, but at least it was warm and damp instead of cold. He straightened up and headed for the wall.

As he finished checking each side, his hope for salvation weakened. No doors. Solid stone blocks along every meter. He cursed the skills of the engineers who'd designed the place.

In the shadows of the far corner he came across a collection of exploration gear, the kind of stuff he'd bring when he was scouting locations for future dig sites. Canteens, a backpack, a climbing rope and some carabiners. The leaves and dirt on them indicated they had been untouched for a while, but not for years. And this was Western gear, not Chinese, definitely not PLA. A sprig of hope shot through his consciousness.

He picked up the pack and rifled through it. Freeze-dried food, extra socks. He touched something hard. He pulled out a blue United States passport. He flipped it open.

The face of Professor Maxwell Carson stared up at him.

He patted down the outside pouches. One had something hard and square in it. He reached in and pulled out a satellite phone.

"Halleluiah! Salvation!"

He pounded the power button. Nothing happened. He flipped the phone over to reveal a wide, corroded crack across the battery compartment.

"Of course," he whispered. "Why have that work out in my favor?"

He carried the pack back to Zhong and Mike.

"Carson was here," he said. "This is his pack."

"I am amazed he survived the dinosaurs to get here," Zhong said.

"I'm not amazed he didn't survive them to get out," Mike said.

"How about a little more enthusiasm that we found a clue to where he is?" Grant said.

"Look, buddy, I know you have this hope to find him alive. But after this long? Without a weapon? He took shelter in the palace one night, headed out the next day, and that was that. You need to admit defeat on the rescue plan and get your head wrapped around a survival plan."

Grant didn't want to give up on Carson. He wanted the old man alive and well and back home dusting off fossils in his study. But he had to admit that while Mike was being a callous jerk about it, from a practical point of view, he could be right.

"No," Grant said. "He left his pack, supplies, and gear in a nice neat pile in a shadowy, hidden place. He would not have continued his dragon search without all of that. And we had to force the main doors open to get in here. Dinosaurs didn't get inside these walls."

"Then a dragon plucked him up and flew off with him," Mike said.

"When he could hide in one of the towers? He wasn't that stupid. He didn't leave this compound."

"I think the soldiers would have found him by now."

Grant looked at the collapsing building in the courtyard center. "Then he must be in the only place where no one has looked."

He pulled his flashlight from his pocket, climbed to the top of the steps, and entered the building. The angle of the sunlight illuminated some of the pit below. The floor was smooth except for a pile of broken marble slabs in the center where the dais floor had collapsed. The missing fourth column lay down there as well, half in shadow. Grant snapped on his flashlight and sent the beam down onto the column.

At the shattered end, a white rope encircled the base. The end trailed off out of sight.

Grant knelt down and peered over the side. A bit of vertigo rippled through him. He cupped his hands around his mouth "Professor Carson?"

Mike stepped up beside him. "What are you doing?"

"He went down there. He tied that rope off to a column, the column broke away, and he couldn't get back out."

"Even if that's true, he couldn't still be alive down there."

Grant had to admit Mike was probably right.

"But there's only one way to find out," Mike said. "I'll go down and check."

CHAPTER TWENTY-FOUR

Grant and Mike began to search the edge of the palace ruin for an anchor point for the climbing rope. Grant did not want to repeat Carson's mistake.

"Where you get that?" Laoxin said from behind him.

Grant turned around to see Laoxin pointing at Carson's pack by the dais.

"That was Carson's. He was here. We think he went down there. We are going to find out."

Zhong walked up carrying the climbing rope. Laoxin looked the three of them in the eyes, as if searching for some kind of subterfuge. She didn't seem satisfied when she didn't find any.

"One go only," she said. She pointed at Mike. "You stay."

"No," Mike said. "I'm the one—"

She called over a soldier and gave him a series of sharp commands. She walked away and the soldier stepped over, rifle across his chest and stood between Mike and the opening.

"Looks like you just volunteered," Mike said to Grant.

"Laoxin told the soldier to kill us if we do anything stupid," Zhong said.

"Make sure he doesn't think coming on this trip qualifies," Grant said.

The first pillar they inspected was dry rotted all along the base, likely the same fatal flaw the missing column had before Carson bet his life on it. But the second seemed solid. Mike looped the rope around it and tossed the rest of the coil over the edge of the opening. It unwound and hit the bottom with plenty to spare. He stepped over to Grant.

"I was ready to go down there," he said.

"Like you'd be much of a climber with that arm," Grant said. He looked over the side. "It's only a few meters down anyway."

Actually, it was about ten meters. And the more Grant looked at it the more he was reminded of the time he barely survived climbing up a rope like this inside an Aztec temple. The memory made him shudder.

He grabbed the rope and shuffled backwards to the edge of the opening. With his feet planted at the lip, he played out the rope between his hands until he was bent into an L shape. His protruding stomach pressed his belt buckle uncomfortably into his groin. He moaned.

"Doing okay?" Mike said.

"Splendid," Grant squeaked.

"Push out, slide down, don't hit your head."

The three bits of advice went nowhere since all Grant could think about was don't crash land and break every bone in his body. He eased himself out another inch and one foot slipped against the jagged edge of the cracked floor.

The rope slithered through his sweat-soaked palms. His heart jumped halfway up his throat as his feet slid off the stone edge. He fell backwards into open space.

In panic, he clamped both hands on the rope. The rushing nylon burned his skin. But with a vision of his skull cracked on the floor below as a motivator, he held tight. He got a grip and stopped his fall. He looked down. A meter and a half to go. One painful handhold at a time, he lowered himself to the floor. His arm muscles quivered at the point of failure. When his feet touched the ground, his knees went weak with relief.

"See," Mike said, "not so bad."

Grant looked at the blisters on his reddening palms. "Not from up there, no."

Using his fingertips, he pulled his flashlight from his pocket and snapped it on. He walked over to the rope and broken column they'd seen from above. Dry rot had been the column's doom, but Carson could never have guessed from looking at the outside of it. Grant played the beam around the area. To the right were the remains of two large wooden buckets. Most of the iron fittings were little but rust, but the huge handles remained, each with a hole in the center for a rope.

He gave the floor and the wall a closer look. This wasn't done in the same block and mortar style of the rest of the structure. This room had a uniform surface, much more like some early form of concrete. Grant stepped back out into the light.

"This isn't a basement," he shouted up. "The walls are sealed and there are the remains of big buckets down here. This was a cistern."

"Any sign of Carson?" Mike said.

"Still looking."

The cistern had a slight uphill slope, though whether by design or accident, Grant wasn't sure. He skirted the rubble in the center and sent his flashlight into the cistern's dark, upper reach. It flashed across something on the floor with a heartbreakingly familiar shape. Grant aimed the beam at the object. A corpse leaned up against the wall.

Grant stepped over to it. The body had been here a while, skin shrunken and gray against the bones. Silver hair covered the scalp and it wore a set of khaki-colored cargo pants and a dark T-shirt. The right foot pointed sideways in a way no right foot ever should. The lower leg of the pants above it was stained black with blood.

In a puddle of water beside the corpse lay a pocket notebook, fuzzy with green mold. Grant picked it up and flipped it open. Blurred ink coated soggy pages. But having spent hours deciphering similar pages over the last few days, he could tell the writing was Professor Carson's special shorthand.

Grant's spirit deflated. He'd come here with one mission, and he'd failed. He would die out here, eaten by a dinosaur, for nothing. He walked back over to the pile of rubble.

"I found Carson's body," he said. "Looks like the column snapped and he broke his leg in the fall and couldn't get back out. Probably bled to death."

"Dammit," Mike said. "Anything useful down there?"

Grant swept the flashlight across the walls. To the left of the corpse was a two-meter circular tunnel that headed up the mountainside. The opening edge was finished in the same style stone as the walls.

"Looks like the cistern didn't fill with rainwater. There's a tunnel heading uphill. Looks like it used to tap into snowmelt or a stream."

"Well, get out of there before the stream decides to refill the place," Mike said.

Grant shuffled back to the dangling rope. With his hands so raw, the climb was going to hurt, even if he thought he had the upper body strength to pull himself up that far.

"The drop down blistered my hands," he said. "Not sure I can make the climb."

"Put a big loop in the rope, stand in it, and the two of us will pull you up." Pause. "Uh, how much do you weigh?"

"You know that a girl never likes questions like that. Just get ready to pull."

Grant tied a big loop in the rope. He stared at the rubble while he waited for the two above him to get ready. He noticed something odd and stepped over to investigate.

A thin layer of black mold seemed to coat the pieces of the floor. But while it was black mold on the upper surface, it was black char on the underside, like the stains on the stones on the inner wall of a fireplace.

How did the Scarlet General manage to light a cistern on fire?

"Ready!" Mike shouted from above.

Grant repositioned the rope and stood on the knot. "Going up. Penthouse, please."

The rope went taut.

Centimeters at a time, Grant rose until he was just under the remains of the floor. He noticed the floor was canted slightly upward all along the edge, which would be the opposite of what would happen with an inward collapse. He let go of the rope and grabbed the floor. The blisters in his hands screamed. The rope went slack and four hands helped pull him up out of the cistern. He collapsed next to Mike and Zhong.

"Thanks," he said. "I couldn't have climbed that rope with these hands." He sat up and sighed.

"Well, we solved the Professor Carson mystery," Mike said.

"But uncovered another one," Grant said. "The collapsed floor in the cistern—"

A shrieking cry from above cut Grant off. Soldiers all along the wall began to shout and point to the sky.

From out of the sun dove an enormous dragon.

CHAPTER TWENTY-FIVE

The dragon tucked its wings like a hawk, extended its front legs forward, and dove like a dart for the palace wall.

The soldiers sent up a storm of bullets from all sides of the palace. But plummeting head-on, the dragon made a narrow target, and it closed on them with the speed of a strafing fighter plane. Most of the rounds seemed to miss, but given how ineffective small arms had been on the dinosaurs, Grant didn't have high hopes they'd make a difference if they hit the dragon.

Tranq-gunners took positions along the sides of the corner towers. It looked like they were planning to dart the thing as it passed over and presented the largest target. They were also less likely to get picked off than the soldiers along the wall. Grant wondered if it was accidental that some of the soldiers had been downgraded to bait.

Grant and the other two dropped down behind the steps to the ruined palace and lay flat on the ground.

A hundred meters out, the dragon spread its wings. With a leathery slap they expanded to a full span and acted like brakes. In a split second, the dragon stopped and hung in mid-air.

A tranq gunner took aim and fired. The dart missed the dragon's body and ripped a hole in its wing like a paper target on a firing range. Then the hole re-sealed.

The dragon sent out a shriek that seemed to rattle Grant's bones. It inhaled and then spat out a stream of orange fire.

Grant's jaw dropped. The whole scene was surreal. A fire-breathing dragon. Self-healing wings. It was like watching a movie.

The jet of fire crashed into the side of the palace walls. Thick flames splattered in all directions. The soldiers ducked behind battlements and most of the fire burst over their heads or ran down the wall's face.

None of the soldiers wanted to take a chance that the dragon's aim would improve. They scrambled in both directions for the towers at the corners of the perimeter wall. With great flaps of its wings, the dragon rose and flew over the palace. The down sweep of its wings ruffled Grant's shirt against his back. The dragon soared skyward.

"The tower!" Mike shouted.

The three bolted for the safety of the closest stone tower. Many of the soldiers had arrived at the same conclusion and were rushing through the door on the battlement.

Halfway there, Grant turned to check on the dragon. He was just in time to see it wheel on one wing and tuck into a second dive, straight for them. They'd never make the tower.

"Get down!" He collapsed against Mike and Zhong's backs and the three of them hit the ground.

The dragon screamed overhead. It let loose a torrent of fire at the bottom of the tower. Flames blew into the opening at the base. The inside lit up like a giant orange lamp. Fire belched from the firing slits at the top. The air filled with the agonizing screams of men roasting alive inside. The door to the top of the wall blew off and spun along the battlements. A soldier, engulfed in flames, staggered out of the doorway and collapsed.

The dragon cut the fire stream, spread its wings, and soared skyward. It let loose a victorious cry.

Grant knew they were all going to die. The dragon was an aerial arsonist and these soldiers had no defense against it. The towers were the only place to hide, and the dragon had just sent one up like a Roman candle.

An idea came to mind.

"The cistern!" he said. "The tunnel will be safe."

Zhong and Mike answered with action, jumped to their feet and ran back to where the climbing rope dangled over the edge of the floor. Mike scooped their packs up on the run and tossed them over the side. Then he plummeted down the rope in a barely controlled free-fall. Zhong climbed down after him.

Overhead, the dragon rotated like a pinwheel and aimed at the palace for a third attack. The surviving soldiers mounted no defense. They streamed to the main gate, apparently preferring death by terrestrial dinosaur than from a flying flamethrower. But the earlier dinosaur attack had bent the crossbar into a curve that wedged the doors closed. Two soldiers hammered at the bar with the butts of their rifles.

Grant grabbed the rope to climb down. His hands squawked a searing reminder that they were blistered as hell from his last attempt at this. He pulled up his shirt and gripped the rope through the cloth. Better, but still painful. It was going to have to do.

He climbed over the side. Above, the dragon had tucked its wings and begun its deadly dive. Grant gripped the rope and winced. He leaned back to go over the edge.

And lost his grip.

In what felt like slow motion, he went over the side and dropped back-first into the cistern. In the sky overhead, a trail of flames shot across the blue as the dragon launched another fiery assault. It didn't matter, though. When his head slammed into the cistern floor, he'd be dead anyway.

The climbing rope tangled around Grant's left leg. The nylon choked Grant's ankle and the rope stretched tight. Now he fell head-first, swinging toward the cistern floor. He didn't have time to react, just to realize he was about to die.

The rope jerked him to a stop. His leg threatened to pop out of his hip. He opened his eyes to an inverted view of the cistern. His hair hung down and the ends brushed the floor. He started a slow upside-down spin.

"What do you know," he said. "Somehow still not dead."

Blood from his pounding heart began to rush to his head and he was sure it was going to explode. He tried to reach up and untie his leg. No luck. For him, doing a normal sit-up was an extreme effort, so doing an upside-down one was an impossibility. He realized there was something worse than cracking his head open on stone and instantly dying: Hanging upside down and being roasted alive by dragon's breath.

Outside above the cistern, men screamed and gunfire erupted. Mike and Zhong ran back to him.

"Stop hanging around here," Mike said.

"Get me out of this before my head turns into a burst balloon."

He reached down and steadied himself against the floor. Mike clamped an arm around Grant's waist and lifted him up a few centimeters. Zhong unwrapped the rope from Grant's ankle. Mike eased him down.

The three dashed for the tunnel at the end of the cistern. Mike grabbed both backpacks en route and everyone clambered into the water pipe. They stopped where shadows turned the tube dark. A slight cool breeze came from up the tunnel.

More men screamed from the palace grounds. Flames splattered into the cistern.

"We're safe," Grant said.

"For now," Mike said. "But if that dragon decides to hop down here and send a jet of fire up the tube, we're barbequed."

"It might even be worse than that," Grant said. "I was checking the collapsed floor. The underside of the debris had been blackened, the edges of the remaining floor turned up. The palace floor didn't collapse from old age and decay. It was blown up and out from the inside."

"Like with a bomb?" Zhong said.

"A steam bomb, maybe," Grant said. "A dragon at the other end of the tube could have sent enough fire down it to set the cistern water to boiling, and then boom."

"That dragon is mopping the floor with us," Mike said. "It doesn't need some secret boiling water plan."

"Sure," Grant said. "It's running over less than a dozen men. But the Scarlet General had a thousand men in the palace. Even a dragon might not want to fly through a flight of a thousand arrows, might come up with a different attack."

"One that requires an understanding of physics?" Mike said.

"It's got a damn big head. Lots of brain case."

From within the palace came more screams from injured men and more bursts of gunfire. The dragon roared and the inside of the cistern lit up orange as torrents of fire crossed the air above it.

"We need to head up this tunnel," Mike said.

"There might be a dragon at the other end," Grant said.

"But there's definitely a dragon at this end."

"He's right," Zhong said.

"It might just fly off," Grant said.

"I'm not betting my life on that bit of wishful thinking," Mike said.

He started to move up the tunnel in a crouch. Zhong was right behind him. Mike clicked on a flashlight.

Grant looked back into the cistern. Something large and immolated dropped into the cistern right at the tunnel entrance. It hit the floor with a thud and a shower of sparks. It was a human body. One charred hand flopped into the tunnel entrance.

Grant recoiled. Then he grabbed his backpack and followed the other two into the dark tunnel.

A great crash echoed in the cistern. A dragon landed in the center, sending bits of stone flying against the walls. Its head darted down and chomped the burning corpse between its jaws. The dragon swallowed and its eyes reddened. Its head turned on its twisting serpentine neck until it looked straight into the tunnel. It screamed.

The cry swept up the tube, amplified as it echoed off the tunnel walls. With it came a blast of hot, humid air that carried the stench of burning flesh.

Grant bolted up the tunnel after the other two, hoping he might outrun the torrent of flame he was certain was seconds away.

CHAPTER TWENTY-SIX

No flames followed them.

A hundred meters up, Mike paused and looked over his shoulder. Zhong and Grant bunched up behind him. Light shone at the tunnel entrance. The dragon appeared to be gone.

"It didn't roast us," Mike said.

"Maybe it couldn't see us in the darkness," Grant said. "Or it opted to conserve whatever allows it to breathe fire since it couldn't get in here to eat us after broiling. No one likes cold food."

"You are certainly quick to give these things credit for intelligence."

"They keep demonstrating it. The attack on the soldiers back there was planned."

Grant took out his flashlight and played it around the tube. The tunnel might have had a finished entrance, but no such care had been taken with the interior. The tube had been hand-hewn and great gouges marred the uneven surface. The floor was a collection of rounded stones. Whether placed there and polished by the flow of water or washed down by whatever once fed the tunnel, Grant could not tell. Their flashlights lit the area a few feet ahead, but no light beckoned them from the other end.

"Wouldn't it be a riot," Grant said, "if the reason the tunnel was dry was that the far end had been blocked off by a landslide?"

Zhong ran his fingers along the scarred tunnel surface.

"My ancestors cut this stone," he said. "Kidnapped by the Scarlet General and enslaved in the darkness until they died. Only to be replaced by more victims."

Mike shouldered his pack. "Let's get out of here."

The tunnel's slope increased as they progressed. Thirty minutes into their hike it became quite steep. Rough steps had been cut into one side and the three men took to climbing them single file. Grant took up the rear, hoping Zhong's slow speed would mask his own. Instead the old man kept up step by step with Mike, and Grant had to struggle to keep up with both of them.

A little while later, the tunnel opened to a sparse forest of squat pine trees. A breeze swirled mist through the trees, obscuring everything over a hundred meters away. They'd climbed into the clouds. The dry stream bed snaked off into the gray.

Grant was happy to see any kind of daylight, no matter how diffused. The breeze injected the mist into his clothing and made him shiver.

"We've climbed into another biome," Grant said.

"Runty pines like this means we're probably up over twelve hundred meters," Mike said.

Grant rested his hands on his knees and breathed deeply. "Funny, doesn't feel like that much of a climb at all."

"This is what my people call the Penjing Forest. The legend says that the dragons' breath burns the tree tops and keeps them from growing tall."

"Or low nutrient levels and colder temperatures stunt the growth," Mike said.

"If my people were forced to dig a tunnel that came to the surface here, I can tell you that they were terrified every moment they stood on this ground."

"I'm with them on that feeling," Grant said. "Now that we've skipped out on our government escorts, let's find a way off this mountain."

"Our best bet would be to find another streambed and follow it down," Mike said.

"Beats crawling through forests," Grant said. He looked around at the mist for the best direction to start their search. "I guess one way is as good as another."

The three began to trek along the mountainside, keeping the upslope side to their left. Up ahead, a dark mass undulated on the ground. The area stank of charred, rancid meat. The three men stopped.

The mass turned out to be a flock of large vultures. One repositioned within the group and displayed a wingspan of over three meters. Unlike the vultures Grant was used to seeing, these had dark brown feathers, with a bald blue-gray head rising from a ruff of shorter neck feathers. The birds pecked and pulled at carrion on the ground.

"Vultures," Zhong said. "Always a bad omen. But I've never seen so many in one place. Usually it's only one or two at a time."

"Maybe one of our dragons died up here," Mike said.

He clapped his hands together loudly and rushed the flock. The birds scattered, but landed just a few meters away, unwilling to completely abandon their feast to the human interloper. Grant and Zhong followed Mike to the vulture's meal.

It wasn't a dragon, or a dinosaur. In fact, the birds hadn't been feeding on one carcass, but many. Two deer lay on the top of the pile, their bodies roasted like they'd been gone over with a blowtorch. Underneath them lay a collection of bones, most not quite picked clean. The skeletons were all different types and sizes, and a casual glance revealed the skulls of other deer, a bear, and a larger ungulate Grant couldn't identify.

"Someone doesn't clean up after meals," Grant said.

"Looks like the dragons feed here," Mike said. "And vultures get the leftovers."

"Which is why there are so many birds together," Zhong said.

"Dragons cook their food," Grant said. "That's a big evolutionary step. Cooking makes digestion easier and makes protein more processable. Man's mastery of fire is believed to have been the spark that allowed us to have the energy to create larger, more complex brains."

"Are you still trying to sell me on dragon intelligence?" Mike said.

"Some birds prepare food by soaking it in water, and you accept that as a sign of intelligence. And what other animal eats in the same location all the time except humans?"

Zhong poked at a skull with a stick. "This is a cow skull. Cows will not wander this far up the mountain through the forest."

Grant looked around the pile of bones. The vultures waiting to return to their meal stood in dinosaur tracks.

"Mike, you saw the dinosaurs before the attack on the cages carrying prey. From the tracks on the ground, it looks like they carried these animals up here."

"And offered it to their dragon god as a sacrifice? Now the dinosaurs are smart as well? Keep crackpot theories like that for your science fiction stories. Dragons fly. They flew down and plucked up a cow. Occam's razor, buddy."

"Maybe so," Grant admitted. "But the dragon pulling the dinosaur out of the pitch lake means there's way more to their relationship somehow."

Two vultures hopped closer and squawked at the men. One beat its wings and bounced up and down.

"I think we've interrupted their meal long enough," Zhong said.

The three moved away from the carrion and the vultures wasted no time returning to devour it.

A half hour later they had yet to find a natural break in the forest worth exploiting to get downhill. Then the smell of charred wood drifted in on the breeze. The idea of a warm campfire appealed to Grant, but the realization that what he sniffed had likely been started by dragon's breath turned that sensation into dread.

Up ahead a tangle of dead branches and uprooted trees rose in an uneven pile. The group stopped beside one of the trees. Grant fingered a dead leaf and ran his hand along the bark.

"These aren't the scrubby pines that grow up here," he said. "These are deciduous hardwoods from lower down on the slopes."

"It would take a hell of a storm to blow them this far uphill," Mike said.

"Even typhoons don't have winds that strong this far inland," Zhong said.

Grant stepped back from one tree trunk and saw that he'd been standing in a dinosaur track. "More evidence that dinosaurs travel up here from the forest. Looks like our dino friends delivered these branches."

They picked their way around the mass. The smell of burned wood turned from comforting to cloying the further they traveled. On the other side, the area opened up to a great mound of steaming charcoal, easily a hundred meters around. The blackened, uprooted stumps of larger trees stuck from the pile at odd angles.

"Dragons holding a marshmallow roast?" Grant said.

"You're the one who thinks they're super smart," Mike said.

Grant lowered a hand to over the top of the charcoal pile. It was warm, but not really hot. Up ahead, slightly obscured by the mist, something lay beside an excavated area of the pile. Grant's scientific inquisitiveness took over and he crossed the charcoal to that spot.

Before he got to the thing that caught his attention, he came across the hole where the charcoal had been dug out for two meters around. Like geologic excavations he was used to, there were layers to the charcoal with different shades and different woods. This process had been going on a long time.

At the base of the pit lay a pile of what looked like broken gray bowls. Grant picked one up. It was a centimeter thick, but surprisingly light. Mike and Zhong joined him at the pit's edge.

"Eggshells," Grant said. "And a lot of them."

"Dinosaurs laid clutches of eggs like that," Mike said.

Grant went to the thing that lay on the ground near the pit. It was a juvenile version of the dinosaurs they had encountered in the forest below. A misshapen head told the tale of some kind of birth defect. It hadn't been dead that long.

"And here's one that didn't make it," Grant said.

"So, dinosaurs climb up this high to lay their eggs?"

"Salmon travel thousands of miles to lay theirs," Grant said. "And maybe this alpine environment is free of some kind of egg-stealing animals that live in the forests."

Off to their left, the charcoal shifted and sent a puff of ashy steam up into the air.

"We're in time to see another one hatching," Mike said.

Mike stepped closer to that spot. Grant held back, his scientific curiosity firmly taking a back seat to his survival instinct this time.

"Do we really want to?" Grant gave the misty expanse around them a useless search. "I mean, what if the mother is waiting on Junior to arrive?"

"Hardly any reptiles look after their young."

"Just alligators, crocodiles, and several snake species. And if these dinosaurs are more related to birds, then that would broaden the list to practically all relatives."

"Do you see any dinosaurs around?"

"I'm standing in a cloud. I can barely see you."

Charcoal near their feet shifted. A little pile swelled and then the charred chunks rolled away to expose the crown of a head and two closed eyes.

"We should not be here," Zhong said.

"I'm siding with Zhong," Grant added.

"It's tiny," Mike said. "It isn't going to hurt you. Damn, this would be worth a fortune."

The eyes opened. Two red slit irises stared at the three men.

"Oh, hell," Grant said.

The rest of the head rose out of the charcoal. The creature shook off the dust and debris and revealed the snout and ears of a scaled down dragon. A pair of wings knifed up through the charcoal behind the head.

"A dragon," Zhong whispered.

The creature opened its mouth and let out a shriek loud enough to make Grant wince.

"The kid has some lungs," Mike said.

Grant's jaw dropped. "Because when it hatches it has to call for—"

From off in the mist came the terrifying reply call of a much larger dragon.

"Its mother," all three men said in unison.

CHAPTER TWENTY-SEVEN

In the open space above the tree line and the obscuring cloud, it was impossible to tell where the adult dragon was. But there was no question that anywhere was too close.

The baby dragon cocked its head at the three humans as if even in its first moments of life the creature knew they didn't belong here. Then it cried out again.

The adult answered, louder than before.

Grant led the two others in a downhill scramble off the smoldering pile. Behind them, the baby dragon crawled up out of the charcoal. It stretched its wings and flapped off a cloud of dark dust.

Just as they cleared the nest, an orange glow seemed to light up the entire cloud around them. Then a blast of heat slammed into Grant's back and the ground behind him burst into flames. The impact knocked the three of them flat to the ground.

The bottom of Grant's feet felt hot. He rolled onto his back and saw the soles of his shoes were on fire. He stomped them against the ground like he was doing some spastic dance. The flames smothered out.

A blurry black shape with outstretched wings appeared in the mist above. It descended and Grant froze where he lay, praying for some kind of divine bequest of invisibility. A dragon came into sharp focus and alighted beside the baby. With a sweep of its head it sent a stream of fire out in a full circle around the charcoal pile. The flames roared over Grant and the others and set fire to the shrubland beyond them.

The tiny dragon looked up at its parent and uttered a plaintive squawk. It ended the cry with its mouth wide open. The dragon positioned its head over the youngster's mouth and regurgitated a nasty red sludge into the little one's gullet. The wretched smell was so strong that Grant had to fight back rising bile. The baby dragon made great, greedy swallows. That only made Grant feel sicker.

Then the adult dragon angled its mouth differently over the tiny dragon's. This time it injected a black slurry. It looked like the oil the dragon had appeared to drink earlier from the pitch lake. The baby's head bobbed back and forth as it ingested the oil. The dragon stopped delivering. The baby closed its mouth, reared back its head, and spit out a small fireball.

The large dragon redirected its attention to the unburned pile of trees and branches the men had first encountered. It let loose a torrent of flame at the base of the pile. The branches burst into a roaring pyre.

The larger dragon then bent down and closed its jaws around the body of its juvenile version, careful to fold its little wings properly to the body. Then it lifted the baby up, and with a few sweeping flaps of its enormous wings, flew off into the mist.

Mike rose to his feet. "That was…incredible."

"A mighty dragon and its young," Zhong said. "All my people's myths are true."

"Which is a good outcome," Laoxin said from behind them.

Grant whirled around to see Laoxin and four soldiers standing near the new bonfire.

"It would be unfortunate for everyone," she said, "if I return without a prize."

CHAPTER TWENTY-EIGHT

"What good news," Grant deadpanned to Laoxin. "We were afraid we'd lost you."

The sarcasm did not translate. "If Americans can escape dragon attack," she said, "so can Chinese soldiers."

The five of them looked like they'd had a harrowing escape. Burned spots mottled their uniforms. A bandage covered one eye and the upper part of one soldier's head. Another's right arm looked uncomfortably like broiled lamb. Soot darkened half of Laoxin's face. Unfortunately for Grant they'd all managed to keep hold of their guns, though none of them had a tranq gun.

"We continue mission," she said.

"Continue mission?" Grant said. "You still think you can capture one of those things armed the way you are? I don't see any tranq guns, and the guns you do have will intimidate the hell out of us, but the apex predators on the mountain treat bullets like mosquito bites."

"Your mission is over," Mike said. "We just need to get off this mountain alive."

Laoxin stamped a foot on the ground. "Mission not over! Cannot return with nothing when dragons here."

Her face lit up. "We bring back eggs."

"What eggs?" Mike said.

"Do not act stupid with me," Laoxin said.

"He's not acting," Grant said.

"We see baby dragon hatch from the ground like sea turtle. We bring back dragon eggs."

"Hang on there," Grant said. "If there are eggs here, we don't know if they are dragon eggs." He pointed to the tiny dinosaur corpse at the edge of the hole dug in the charcoal. "There were dinosaur and dragon eggs in this nest. Even though technically, I think they were all the same eggs to start with."

"I do not understand," Zhong said. "Two different animals."

"Eventually, yes," Grant said. "But there are reptile species that transform in the egg depending on external factors like temperature. Alligator gender depends on how warm the soil is while the baby is developing. The fact that the dragon emerged far from the dinosaur could mean that the dragons or dinosaurs or both tending this nest did something different to the dragon area, perhaps keeping it at a different temperature by dragons re-firing the charcoal."

"Yeah," Mike said. "But with alligators, you still get an alligator, not another species."

"Bees have workers, drones, and queens in a hive. All functionally different, all the same species. Sexually dimorphic creatures are common, many with only one gender having wings."

"So female dinosaurs and male dragons?" Mike said.

"It's possible. The skins of both are identically textured. And which is more likely, two extinct species surviving on a mountain in China, or just one?"

"And the dragons *are* ingesting that petrochemical soup from the oil ponds. That would sure speed up some genetic reprogramming. But genders having opposite sleep cycles seems counterproductive for reproduction."

"Hey," Grant said. "If humans had that schedule I'd probably still be married to my ex-wife."

"Stop conversation," Laoxin said. "No care what comes out of egg as long as PLA scientist see it hatch. We bring back eggs. You three find eggs."

"We don't have shovels," Grant said.

"You have hands." Laoxin drew her pistol from her holster. "Find eggs."

She gave the soldiers a brusque order in Chinese. They circled the charcoal pile with their rifles trained on the three men.

"I really only do this at Easter," Grant said, "but I'll make an exception since you asked so nicely."

He and the other two dropped to their knees and began to sift through the charcoal. The going was tough, and warm.

"You catching the heat this charcoal has retained?" Mike said.

"Warmer when you go deeper," Grant said. "Dragons have to be tending these nests, relighting them regularly to keep the eggs at the right temperature."

"Perhaps those are the flashes of light we see from the village up on the mountain," Zhong said.

"Still think they aren't smart?"

"Penguins tend nests," Mike said, "And they're literally bird brains."

A finger-tingling half hour later, the three had hand-sifted the nest and found nothing but broken egg shells.

"There's nothing here," Grant said to Laoxin. "The eggs have all hatched."

Laoxin pointed to the burning pyre of logs. "Eggs are in there."

"You do see the flames, right? Unless you brought a fire extinguisher, there's no way we get in there until that burns itself down. And that's if a dragon doesn't come back and relight the thing."

"We find other nests. Follow dinosaur tracks."

Several sets of tracks led up the mountain through the sparse trees. Laoxin gave the soldiers some orders and they herded Grant and the others to the dinosaur trail. One soldier poked Mike with the barrel of his rifle to get him walking uphill.

"Looks like we get to break trail," Mike said.

"The hospitality here is never ending."

CHAPTER TWENTY-NINE

The soldiers allowed Grant and the others a healthy lead as they followed the dinosaur tracks up the mountain, apparently more than willing to let them encounter any dragons first.

"You know," Mike said, "even with my impending death possibly only seconds away, I can't help but marvel at these dragons/dinosaurs/whatever they are. Based on our observations, I think the dragons are diurnal and the dinosaur nocturnal."

"We haven't seen dinosaurs in daylight," Grant said. "And their large eyes seem to be night adapted. We've only seen dragons in daylight. It would certainly be more efficient if the two types hunted the mountain at different hours."

As they climbed, the air chilled and the cloud dissipated. Soon they were above the cloud layer and the sun blazed in a bright blue sky. Only a few patches of scraggly trees broke up the open, rocky expanse. The mountain's peak rose just ahead of them. The dinosaur tracks ran in that direction.

"This place has zero cover if dragons attack," Mike said.

"Thanks for that observation," Grant said. "Silly me was only worried about the lack of food and water and the risk of hypothermia."

A breeze from up ahead brought the scent of oil and burned wood with it.

"I think I can smell a nest up ahead," Zhong said.

"Once we get the eggs off the mountain," Grant said, "what are the odds Laoxin lets us go?"

"I think you know the answer to that question," Zhong said.

Up ahead, something littered the ground. When they got closer, the items became discernable. Hundreds of ancient Chinese battle helmets lay all over the ground. Around the helmets lay tarnished and mangled battle armor. Zhong gasped and knelt beside one helmet. A skull still filled the helmet.

"The end of the Scarlet General's army," Zhong said. "Destroyed by dragons."

The soldiers caught up with them. The sight of the remains of the defeated army sent them into rapid, nervous chatter. Laoxin stepped up and snapped at them. They went silent.

"They are afraid," Zhong said. "This is a very bad omen. They fear that the spirits of the dead still haunt this place."

"I'm still thinking dragons are a bigger problem," Grant said.

"Laoxin chastised them for having peasant superstitions."

"Yesterday, dragons were peasant superstitions."

"Get moving!" Laoxin shouted. "Time is wasting."

Mike led the three further up the mountain. They came across another broad pile of charcoal. Steam rose from the mound's center and the pile appeared undisturbed. At the edge of the pile, Mike dropped his pack to the ground.

"Find eggs," Laoxin said.

The three men headed into the nest. The soldiers surrounded them again. This time the soldiers didn't direct all their attention to the men on the pile. Now they watched the sky as well.

Grant knelt down and dug into the charcoal. After a few minutes, he uncovered a gray, curved surface. Part of him hoped that it was just another broken shell, since finding intact eggs meant the end of his usefulness to Laoxin. But the scientist in him couldn't help but be excited at the chance to hold an intact egg, knowing that inside lay the embryo of a link to the planet's past.

He swept the charcoal away. The egg was still intact. He carefully dug out all around it. The egg was about the size of two grapefruits. He lifted it up into the daylight. Inside, he felt a very developed hatchling scurry in a circle.

He nearly dropped the egg in shock. He was actually holding a living link to the dinosaurs he'd always studied in his hands.

Laoxin rushed over. "Success!"

She grabbed the egg from Grant's hands.

"Hey, careful!" Grant said. "The egg is more fragile than you think."

Laoxin barked at one of the soldiers. He ran over and shed the pack from his back. She turned it upside down and dumped its contents on the nest. She snapped another order at the soldier and he shed his uniform shirt as well. Clad only in a sleeveless T-shirt, he shivered in the cold air. Laoxin wrapped the egg in the man's shirt and placed it in the backpack.

"I found one," Zhong said.

He pulled an egg from the nest. Laoxin went to him and ordered another soldier to shed his shirt. She wrapped the second egg in his shirt and put it in the pack. She marched over to Mike, whose hands were buried several centimeters deep into a pile of charcoal.

"Where your egg?"

"There's nothing here," he said. "Well, except what I think from the smell of it is dragon poop."

He reached over and grabbed a handful of what did look like black-brown excrement, excreted at a dragon-level amount. He held it up to Laoxin.

"Your scientists might want—"

Laoxin recoiled at the smell and turned away, "Drop that before I shoot you."

Mike dropped it. Laoxin fastened the backpack closed and walked it over to the shirtless soldier in the middle. He put the backpack on. She shouted something triumphant at the soldiers.

"She says now we go home and get rich," Zhong translated.

From above them came the shriek of a dragon.

"I don't think Dad likes that plan," Grant said.

CHAPTER THIRTY

A dragon dove down at them from out of the sun.

Grant, Zhong, and Mike scattered from the nest and into a patch of scrubby pines. Grant weighed a continued sprint against hiding. His heaving lungs voted to hide. He nestled in-between two trees.

The soldier with the eggs shed his backpack as they all pointed their guns at the descending dragon. The men sent a spray of bullets into the air. Rounds ripped through the dragon's wings and bounced off its body with no effect. As the dragon closed on the group the soldiers scattered, save one terrified soul standing frozen on the charcoal nest. The dragon landed rear legs first on him.

The creature's weight drove the soldier down into the nest and he disappeared into the sea of charcoal. The dragon flapped its wings and rose from the ground. It pulled the soldier from the nest and he immediately began screaming. While still in mid-air, the dragon whipped its neck around and with its jaws, snapped off the head of the soldier. It dropped onto the nest and rolled away.

The other two soldiers shuddered at the sight of their decapitated comrade and stared at the corpse.

Laoxin screamed an order at them and began to shoot at the dragon's head. The other two joined in, apparently also aiming at the head. But a smaller target and rattled nerves meant that few of the bullets hit the mark. Without a detailed analysis, Grant couldn't be sure that a lucky eye shot would even kill the dragon the way it had a dinosaur. And he had no intention of getting that up close and personal with a dragon.

The dragon flinched as several rounds struck its head. Its eyes reddened and it turned to the closest soldier. Under the dragon's gaze, the soldier's jaw dropped and his rifle fell to his side.

The dragon reared back and then projectile sprayed a tube of fire at the soldier. The impact picked the man up off his feet and sent him flying backwards fifty meters. When the dragon cut the flow, a trail of fire led from the nest to a corpse that had already been reduced to near ash.

That was enough for the remaining soldier. He broke and ran downhill. Laoxin ran off to the left.

The dragon pursued the soldier. This time it just ran. Charging with alligator-like speed it crushed any trees in its way as it bolted after the soldier. Dirt and charcoal flew backwards with every flying step. The soldier screamed in such a panicked high pitch that the sound hurt Grant's ears.

The dragon caught up. It raised its left front foot and swiped the soldier to the ground. With a jab of its head it clamped its jaws around the man's midsection, and then lifted his screaming form up off the ground. With a crunch, the soldier went silent and limp. Blood rushed out over the dragon's lower jaw. With another crunch, the top and bottom of the soldier fell to the ground. The dragon tossed back and swallowed the midsection still in its mouth. Then it turned its attention to the fleeing Laoxin.

It extended its wings and with one flap, jumped to right behind her. The dragon landed with a crash and reduced several trees to splinters. It screamed after Laoxin.

She decided to go down swinging. Laoxin stopped and spun around to face the dragon. Aiming her pistol at its head, she fired until her magazine was empty. She ejected the magazine and slapped a new one home. She fired one more ineffective round, and then in frustration, she threw the empty gun on the ground. As she waved her arms at the creature, Laoxin shouted something that sounded like daring the creature to kill her.

The dragon turned sideways and with a flick of its tail, it sent the armored spade at the tail's tip sailing at Laoxin. Before she could react, the tail had flicked across her chest. Red blossomed along a thin slash left along the tail's path.

Laoxin staggered forward. Shock froze her face. Then her chest cavity opened like an enormous second mouth. Internal organs poured out in a rush. She grabbed them with her hands to try and hold them inside. Her eyes rolled up in her head and she fell forward, hitting the ground face-first. She didn't move.

The dragon surveyed the battlefield of its victory. Grant froze behind the tree, hoping that being downwind of the creature would help him and the other two remain undiscovered. The dragon huffed and sauntered over to the rucksack containing the eggs. It sniffed several times over the bag. Then it tore open the bag with its claws. Two eggs rolled out.

Then the dragon nosed them back into the open rucksack. It scooped the whole bag into its mouth and lightly closed its jaws. Then it launched itself into the air and flew away toward the mountain's peak.

As soon as he was sure the dragon wasn't going to circle back, Grant stood up and shouted for the other two. Mike and Zhong stood up from behind two boulders. They met by the empty nest.

"That's officially as close to a dragon as I need to get," Grant said. "Mike, you're sure no one survived from the base camp?"

"Absolutely."

"Then we just need to dodge the wildlife to get out of here. Zhong, think you can guide us down the mountain and back to your village?"

"It will take days," he said. "Maybe we travel during daylight to avoid the dinosaurs."

"I have a quicker route," Mike said.

He led the other two over to Laoxin's corpse. She looked like a broken egg; two halves split apart at an odd angle with a puddle of stinking organs exposed in the middle.

Mike searched through Laoxin's pack. He smiled in triumph and pulled out her satellite phone.

"All right!" Grant said. "Scotty, beam us up!"

Mike grabbed Laoxin's pistol from the ground and pointed it at Grant.

"Sorry, Redshirts," Mike said. "Only one of us is going home."

CHAPTER THIRTY-ONE

"Mike?" Grant said. "What the hell are you doing?"

"Getting home and getting rich," he said.

"You don't have to kill us to get that done."

"And for old time's sake, I really hope you're right. So don't try to do anything stupid to stop me. Because much as I value our friendship, I value my departure from this mountain even more. You two just have a seat."

Grant and Zhong sat down. Mike kept the pistol trained on them as he dialed the satellite phone.

"Sometimes it isn't just the rocks that teach hard lessons," Mike said to Grant.

The satellite phone rang on the other end and someone picked up.

"It's me. Ready to get picked up." Pause. "No, I *wish* I was in Chengdu. Check the GPS locator. I'm on a mountaintop near the village of Zhōng Xiū." Pause. "Yeah, I know there's no airfield. We'll use the rig. How long until you'll be on station?" Pause. "Roger that. Ready in three-zero minutes."

Mike hung up the phone.

"All righty, then," he said to Grant and Zhong. "Time for you two to get to work."

"You can't get out of here," Grant said. "There's no place for a plane to land."

"It won't have to. It will just fly by and pick me up like a train used to pick up sacks of mail. And you two are going to set up the rig for me. And once I'm gone, you two can hike back down the mountain to freedom."

"If we can avoid dragons, dinosaurs, and the PLA," Grant said.

"Are you trying to make the empathetic case for me shooting you instead? If so, you're doing a great job."

"No, we'd like to leave with you. Drop us off anywhere but here when you're done."

"Sorry, the rig is built for one. You should have brought your own. Remember Rule #3?"

Under gunpoint, Mike led them down the barren hill to the remains of the Scarlet General's army. There they found four metal pikes that had survived the general's calamitous defeat. They carried them back up to the crest of the mountain where Mike directed them to lash them together top to bottom in sets of two, using short sections of rope from his pack. The extended pikes now rose over four meters high.

Mike extracted a harness from his pack. It had heavy red canvas straps like an over-designed safety harness with two longer straps attached to the shoulders. He laid it on the ground and directed Grant and Zhong to implant the two poles a few meters on either side. Mike had them hook the hanging straps from the harness to a loop of rope. Then they stretched the loop between the top of the poles.

"What exactly did we just construct?" Grant said.

"My escape plan," Mike said. "In a few minutes, a vintage DC-3 flies overhead. A hook hanging from below it snags the rope between the poles. I'm in the harness when it does, and off I fly like Superman."

"That's crazy," Zhong said.

"I've done it before. With the same aircraft and pilot. Piece of cake."

"This plan makes you a thief *and* a lunatic," Grant said. "But how does it make you rich?"

"I liked Laoxin's plan so much, that I appropriated it for myself."

Using his foot, he nudged open the backpack at his feet. Inside, lay a dinosaur egg.

"You *are* crazy," Zhong said.

"Didn't you see what just happened to Laoxin?" Grant said.

"Because she had two eggs with her. And I may have added some dragon poop to her bag just to amp up the scent. By the time that dragon gets its senses clear enough to sniff another missing egg, he'll have to be able to fly up about 10,000 meters to get a hold of it."

"Look man," Grant said. "Skip over all the ethical bridges you're burning here. Just for the sake of science, the reason we got into this thing to begin with, don't do this. Obviously, the eggs are under a specific temperature control regimen by the dragons. That egg, out of the ground, then up in a cold plane at altitude for hours. There's no way the hatchling inside is going to survive."

"Doesn't matter to me. I've been buying for a group of off-the-grid scientists cloning mammoths and Ice Age wolves. They're doing wonders with frozen DNA. This will be like making Dolly the Sheep. We'll be ranching these things in six months."

"Dragons will roast you all."

"Looks like if they don't drink tar, they can't make enough fire to light a candle. Fire problem solved."

"But if—"

"Oh, shut up," Mike said. "I need your moralizing like I need a dragon breath enema. You ivory tower profs love to wax on about pure science from your tenured jobs where you teach class a few hours a week. Well, the rest of us have to scramble to break even. I could have been like you, but everyone conspired against me and locked me out of that world. Well, there were people out there with as much appreciation for the extinct as all of you had, and the money to back it up. I cater to their needs, and I don't need to apologize for it to you or anyone else."

He lifted the egg out of the backpack and gave it a kiss. "This is my Golden Ticket, my buried treasure, my sweepstakes winner, all rolled up into one."

The egg shuddered in his hands. A crack formed along the top.

"Well," Mike said. "Looks like it's Junior's birthday. Damn, now I'll have to kill it before pickup."

The top of the egg cracked again. An irregular circle of shell fell away to reveal a dark interior.

"Wonder if we got a dragon or a dino?' Mike said.

He peered into the egg.

A dragon's head shot out of the top of the egg, jaws wide open. Rows of tiny, razor-sharp teeth clamped onto both sides of Mike's neck. Blood spurted like a fountain as Mike screamed in pain. He dropped the egg, but the dragon held on, a determined predator at hatching.

Mike dropped his gun and grabbed the dragon with both hands, but the slick remnants of the egg sac made it impossible to get a grip on the writhing creature. The dragon curled its spine and sank the claws of its rear feet into Mike's chest. Rib bones cracked. Mike's wail went to a higher pitch and he fell backwards onto the ground. One final pulse of rich, red blood sprayed into the air, and Mike went still.

Grant and Zhong had been stunned into motionlessness. Now Grant feared running and introducing the dragon to its second kill.

"I wouldn't move," Grant whispered.

"I'm not sure that I could," Zhong said.

The dragon tore Mike's neck out in one jerk. It chewed twice and then swallowed. Blood coated the sides of its jaws. Then it raised its eyes to the sky, opened its mouth, and screamed.

"Oh, no," Grant said.

From somewhere down the mountain, an adult dragon shrieked a response.

CHAPTER THIRTY-TWO

"Now we're running," Grant said.

Without any thought process, Grant turned and ran uphill while Zhong skidded downhill. As soon as his huffing and puffing convinced him of the error of his decision, the leathery sound of great flapping wings filled the air. An enormous shadow passed over Grant and he did not need to turn around and see what cast it.

The baby dragon cried out in a plaintive wail. The adult dragon screamed so loudly Grant felt it echo inside his skull. He scrambled up to a boulder on the hillside and dove behind it.

Below him, Zhong had disappeared. He took that as a good sign. If he couldn't see the old man, maybe neither could the dragon. The dragon spread its wings like two huge air brakes and landed beside the baby. The baby jumped onto the adult's leg and held on with four feet worth of claws. The adult dragon roared and batted the youngster down with its head.

The dragon lay down a ring of fire around the area where the baby stood. Flames shot five meters into the air. Then the dragon eyed Grant behind the boulder. Its eyes narrowed and reddened.

"Hell, no."

The dragon spat balls of flames in Grant's direction. He ducked behind the boulder and prayed.

Fireballs blasted the ground to his left and right. Rock and earth exploded into the air and then another surge of flames swelled from both sides.

Downhill, the dragon shrieked again. Grant hazarded a look around the boulder just in time to see the adult dragon drop its head and snatch the baby off the ground. It spread its wings, crouched, and then launched itself into the sky. The force of its wings snuffed some of the flames around the poles and the pickup rig.

But not the flames to Grant's right and left. The dragon's fireball attack had blasted open new seeps of liquid tar. Boiling liquid filled the air with choking, toxic fumes. All across the mountainside, cracks opened in the earth, and the black liquid in each crevice quickly turned red and then burst into flames.

The raucous clatter of ancient piston engines sounded from the east. Up in the sky the sun glinted off the fuselage of a fat little DC-3 as it turned to make an approach to the empty pickup rig.

In his long history of entertaining bad ideas, one of the worst came to mind. He needed a way off this mountain before one of several forms of grisly death overtook him. There was a plane ready to make that happen. All he had to do was wrap a few canvas straps around himself, and let an airplane snatch him off the ground.

Mike had called it a piece of cake.

There was a problem, though. Either a view of a burning mountainside or an empty rig would be more than enough to have the mercenary aircraft skip this mission and head home. Which would leave him with choices of death by burning tar, flaming dragon, or stomping dinosaur. None of those options thrilled him.

The earth beneath his feet shifted. He looked down to see he'd been surrounded by a ring of red-hot tar. The patch of ground he stood on now floated like a tiny ice flow on a sea of burning petrochemicals. And the edges were crumbling.

He climbed up atop the boulder. The pickup rig was just a few meters downhill. To his left, the DC-3 had leveled its wings, but not in alignment with the rig. The pilot apparently wasn't keen on roasting his plane for nothing.

Grant judged the distance to the rig. If he jumped off the boulder, he could hit the ground short of a steaming crevice, jump to the left, and then if he rolled on one shoulder—

The mountain decided he didn't need a plan. The boulder shifted under his feet. He lurched forward and tumbled head-first for the ground. His rotund center of gravity forced his body into a life-saving sideways shift. He hit the ground on his left shoulder instead of his face.

Momentum took control and sent him on a spin downhill like a rolling log. Dirt and stone poked and sanded him at every contact. He rolled over the now red crevice in the ground at just the right speed to give his neck the kind of searing treatment he preferred saved for a tuna steak. Just as the pain registered, he bounced up and through the diminished ring of fire around the recovery rig. He bounded to a stop against Mike's backpack.

He took a deep breath. He felt broiled, but not actively burning.

"Somehow," he said to himself, "still not dead."

He dug through the pack until he found the satellite phone. He pressed redial with his bloody, toasty finger. The other phone rang twice.

"I swear to God, if I go to voicemail…"

Someone in the aircraft picked up. "Mike?"

Grant wasn't in the mood for an explanation as to who he was. "Yeah," he grunted. "Don't leave me here, you bastards."

He hoped that sounded Mike-like enough.

"That you by the rig? The mountain's all on fire and the clouds are closing in."

Grant looked downhill. Indeed a San Francisco-worthy wall of fog crawled upslope.

"Strap in now," the voice said, "or we're heading back without you."

Grant dropped the phone and jumped at the harness. He had no idea how to put it on. The long straps hung clipped to the rope loop by two carabiners. It looked like his legs should go through the two loops at the bottom.

Above him, the plane's engines throttled up to a roar. One wing dipped as it headed for the rig.

Grant stepped into the loops. A big strap ran across his chest, split into a Y below his neck, and connected to the straps that ran to the rope loop. A bewildering octopus of other straps and clips seemed to hang from random parts of the rig

Grant just started pulling and snapping straps in place. Reaching behind him, reaching below him, pulling across his back, cinching around his chest. Any clip that could reach any D-ring got connected. No straps were symmetrical. No fit was comfortable. But he looked around left then right, and at least there wasn't any strap left over.

The plane roared again as it powered up to sweep him off the ground. He couldn't see it. He looked over his shoulder. It was approaching from behind. He looked at the recovery rig with an epiphany of new understanding.

He had it on backwards.

Instead of being picked up with the plane flying at him, and his back to the wind as they pulled him up, he'd be smacked in the face with a hundred-plus mile per hour slipstream.

He didn't think the bungee cord holding his glasses on was rated for sitting in a hurricane. But there was no time to worry about it.

The DC-3 roared in so low Grant wondered if it would decapitate him and save him the horror of execution by windburn. A big grappling hook hung from a thick rope below the plane. Grant faced away from the plane, tucked his head, closed his eyes, and waited to die.

The plane thundered over his head and made his fillings vibrate. The huge hook swished by and caught the rope ring in the center. Before he knew what was happening, the plane yanked Grant off the ground.

The harness gave him a super-atomic wedgie and confirmed the fact that he did indeed have it on backwards. His right arm also seemed a few millimeters from coming out of its socket. But the tornado-force wind in his face made the rest of his discomfort immaterial. He thought he could feel layers of his skin peeling away.

Below him, the ground slipped farther away, and above, the plane drew closer. The pilot was climbing and they were reeling him in. In a few minutes, this would all be over. He could bear this a little while longer.

Then he started to spin.

Grant had never been much of a spinner. No Mad Hatter Tea Cups at Disneyland, no merry-go-rounds, no stirring his coffee too quickly. Spinning always ended in vomit.

He gripped the straps over his head and closed his eyes. That only made the sensation worse. And the spin accelerated. He wondered how ice skaters didn't throw up after every double axel.

He remembered that ice skaters tucked in their arms to spin faster. Maybe he should do the opposite.

The idea of letting go of the straps and just hanging in the harness ran counter to common sense. But he let go and stretched out his arms. The spinning slowed. He angled his hands, the way he had when he was a kid sticking them out a moving car window to have the air current make them rise and dive. He managed to stay straight, sailing along under the aircraft, arms outstretched like an albatross. He looked down at the ground.

Fear of heights added to his centrifugal nausea. Now he knew death was certain. It was just a question of whether he'd first throw up all of his internal organs or have a heart attack.

He finally made it to the fuselage. The cable ran through a boom outside the big open door along the side. A crew member stuck his head out the door as Grant closed on the boom. The crewman had a long beard, a shaved head, and giant holes in his earlobes. This was the man who was going to save Grant's life?

Grant made it just short of the boom and the cable stopped reeling in. The crewman reached out and grabbed Grant's arm. He yanked him into the plane. Another crewman released the cable brake. Crewman Earlobes unhooked the extraction rig and then stared at Grant.

"You're not Mike."

"Mike couldn't make it."

Grant teetered a bit and wasn't sure if it was from the aircraft moving or his inner ear still reacting to the Spin of Death on the way up.

"He paid in advance for one extraction. You. Him. All the same to me."

"Where are we extracting to?"

"Singapore. Sound good?"

"Anywhere but China," Grant said.

The nausea inside him finally boiled over. He lay on the floor of the plane and hung his head out the open door, and let a stream of puke out to paint the side of the aircraft. In the aftermath, he felt wonderful.

Through bleary eyes he looked back at the Forest of Fire just in time to see clouds advance over the top. A black dragon's wing pierced the top of the cloud cover like a shark fin at sea, then disappeared into the gray. Then down where the cloud met the tree line on the mountainside, an orange glow flared and disappeared.

No one would ever believe what he'd just been through.

CHAPTER THIRTY-THREE

Two days later.

Grant dropped his bag on his office floor and collapsed at his desk. He'd made it back to Robeson University from Singapore with time for a shower at home and forty minutes to spare before his first class after Thanksgiving break. He'd survived fire-breathing dragons, but was now convinced jet lag and a lack of sleep would surely kill him.

Dean Malley knocked on Grant's open door and stepped in at the same time. Grant sighed. The last thing he wanted right now was to deal with the dean.

"Professor Coleman, I see you survived."

Grant sat up. He wondered just what the dean knew about his recent illegal trip to China.

"Survived?" Grant said.

"Thanksgiving break, the inevitable overeating, the family-induced stress."

Grant relaxed. "Yes. Survived it all."

"But missed the special morning staff meeting."

Dammit. Grant had completely forgotten about it.

"I'm sorry. I forgot that it was scheduled."

The dean gave Grant a disdainful once over. "I have to say, from the looks of you, it seems lucky you remembered to come in at all. I suppose you were writing one of your little stories over the break."

"Mostly research. Thinking about setting it in China."

"The University has donors from around the world. Take care not to write anything that would offend any of them."

"I wouldn't dream of it."

"It's bad enough your genre stories are associated with our department to begin with. Don't let writing them jeopardize your position here."

Dean Malley turned and left the office, which was a good thing since the sarcastic response on the tip of Grant's tongue definitely would have jeopardized his position at the university.

He turned on his computer to check his emails. Days' worth of messages rolled up on the screen. One of them had Chinese characters as the sender's name. He'd normally delete it as instant spam, but the title said GREETINGS FROM ZHONG. That made his heart race. He'd worried about what happened to Zhong from the moment they'd separated on the mountain. The message had arrived late last night. The name and the timing were too much of a coincidence. He opened the email. The message read:

From Zhong about your Forest of Fire visit.

There was a video attachment. Grant clicked on it.

The video player opened. Zhong sat in his shop with a display of canned goods behind him.

"I am sending you this video so you know the message is from me. I've sent it through a third party for security reasons, so I am sorry you cannot reply to it. But again, for security reasons that is probably best as well.

"You can see that I made it back down the mountain after the incident."

Grant had to laugh at the use of the word incident to describe days of dinosaur and dragon attacks.

"I told the soldiers in the village that Laoxin and her soldiers had wiped themselves out in a mutiny inspired by Laoxin's instability. We found no dragons but she insisted the soldiers continue with no supplies and in increasingly dangerous pursuits, even after most were killed by a bomb she ordered dropped on her own soldiers. I said I was lucky to escape with my life. They believed me."

Hearing Zhong was safe and sound was a great relief to Grant.

"The government has discredited Laoxin and her crazy dragon theories," Zhong continued, "and the people of my village have been left in peace. There will be no more dragon hunting here. I believe that you will do all in your power to help us maintain our peace."

"You bet, Zhong," Grant whispered to the screen. "As far as I'm concerned, the creatures in the Forest of Fire will always be a secret."

CHAPTER THIRTY-FOUR

Six months later.

Like a rare planetary alignment, in the month of June, everything seemed to line up in Grant's favor.

The college semester ended with Grant getting some grudgingly positive feedback from Dean Malley. One of Grant's graduating students landed a nice position at the Smithsonian, in part from Grant's glowing recommendation. That student's wealthy father had donated a tidy sum to the Paleontology department in appreciation for the fine job they did instructing his son. It killed Malley to have to thank Grant, which doubled how great Grant felt about the whole thing.

The second big event was the sale of another book. *The Forest of Fire* was a completely fictional account of a professor in China finding dragons. His publisher loved it, and said he hoped Grant never ran out of inspirations for his amazing stories. Grant didn't tell him that he really hoped he did before his "inspirations" managed to kill him.

The advance for that book meant that his monthly dues to the Ex-Wife Party Fund were up to date and even two months ahead. That meant no big bills to pay during summer break when his college paychecks paused.

And to put icing on the Grant Happiness cake, he'd been invited on a paleontological dig in Utah with another university, all expenses paid as a consultant. That started in July.

Every star in the sky seemed to shine on Grant Coleman right now.

He was celebrating and treating himself to a two-week trip to Hawaii. Not the tourist mecca of Oahu, but the Big Island, where the pace was more relaxed and he could visit Volcanoes National Park and see Kilauea volcano up close and personal. Just not too up close.

Grant was all smiles as he checked in at the airport for the first of several legs that would transport him to paradise. He wore an outrageously bright Hawaiian shirt for the occasion, a pair of tan cargo shorts, and a ridiculous straw Panama hat. He even paid the extra fee to check his bag, putting his fear of the airline losing it behind the feeling of freedom by not dragging it around. Then he breezed through security and found himself with enough time for a coffee and a cinnamon roll before he had to board his flight. The day could not get better.

Just prior to boarding, Grant decided to use the men's room and see if he could avoid subjecting himself to the confines of an aircraft restroom during his flight. On his way in, he passed one man on his way out. There wasn't anyone else there. He stood at a center urinal and proceeded with business.

Two men in dark suits and sunglasses entered the bathroom. They had the builds of NFL linebackers.

One of them stopped in the doorway and slid a CLOSED FOR CLEANING sign into place. The other headed for Grant.

Whatever was about to go down, Grant wanted nothing to do with it. He cut his business off midstream and tried to zip his pants back up. The zipper stuck. He yanked it twice to no avail. Knowing he was running out of time, he turned to leave with his fly open. He practically ran into the man in the suit.

"Whoa, excuse me." Grant stepped sideways.

The man moved to block him.

"Doctor Coleman," the man said. It sounded more like an accusation.

"Me? No. My name's Jack. Just a random vacationer. My flight's boarding and I really have to—"

The man grabbed Grant at both shoulders. It felt like if he exerted a newton more pressure, Grant's bones would break. He squeezed in and Grant wasn't going anywhere.

The other man left his station at the doorway. He pulled a large syringe from inside his coat and pulled the cap off the needle with his teeth.

"Oh my God. How did you get that past TSA?"

The man stepped beside Grant and aimed the needle at Grant's neck.

"Look, really, whatever this is, it's a mistake," Grant said. "I don't even know—"

The needle plunged into Grant's neck with all the finesse of a prisoner shivving a guard. Before he could react to the pain, his body went limp. Then the lights in the room went dim, and then went out.

***

Grant woke up on a cold metal floor. The high noise level and the slight jostling told him he was on an airplane. He guessed it wasn't going to Hawaii. He cleaned some dirt from his glasses. There were crates around him. Most of the stencils on the outside were in foreign languages.

He got to his feet and had to hold on to a crate to keep his balance. Whatever the agent of evil in the restroom had injected him with hadn't quite worn off.

He staggered to the front of the aircraft. Three people sat against the bulkhead. None looked happy. The young woman in the group wore jeans, a blue golf shirt with a company logo on the chest and heavy-duty work boots. Her short blonde hair was suffering from a severe case of bed head. She looked up at Grant.

"Well, Sleeping Beauty is finally awake."

"Where am I?"

"On a plane flying to the Arctic Circle with the rest of the kidnapped."

"What the hell for?"

"Don't you know? We're on our way to capture wooly mammoths."

The End

AFTERWORD

Well, looks like Grant survived another adventure. Is this guy pressing his luck, or what?

At the conclusion of Curse of the Viper King, Grant needed to embark on a new adventure. All of the news stories about amazing fossil finds in China made that the natural location to attract a paleontologist.

The current tsunami of discoveries began in the mid-1990s, in Sihetun, when a farmer discovered the earliest known feathered dinosaur, later named *Sinosauropteryx* ("the China dragon bird"). Since then, the region has yielded more than forty dinosaur species, including *Yutyrannus*, a 3,100-pound feathered dinosaur, and *Anchiornis huxleyi*, a rooster-size creature well preserved enough to determine feather colors. The biggest finds are from the middle-late Jurassic period, 166 million years ago, and the Cretaceous, from 131 million to 120 million years ago. The later era has yielded twenty-four species of the winged reptiles called pterosaurs. How could I write about a paleontologist and not have him end up in China?

There are frequently many science nuggets in my books which are true. Dragons (except for Komodo, sea, and snap versions) are definitely not. Much as we all would love to live in the world of *Reign of Fire*, it can't happen. Attaching wings (fifth and sixth appendages) to any species and expecting it to fly is a real stretch, mechanically. There's also the issue of density. Creatures that fly are by necessity very light. Something that travels across the ground and hunts has to have strong bones and powerful muscles. These two versions of animals don't mix. Thank God. I prefer we remain the apex predator on the planet.

The dinosaurs and the dragons are very different versions of the same animal. As Grant points out, bees do this with three different versions all coming from the same hive and queen. In the story the split is along gender lines, and there are many examples in nature where genders have significant differences. Size differences are common, having the male be much smaller or much larger than the female. Black widow spiders are an extreme example. Males are less than half the size of females, and have only one twelfth the life span. If the female does not eat him after sex, that is.

In the story it appears that the dinosaurs are bringing food to the dragons. Before you email labeling me a sexist for having women make the meals, this behavior is modeled off lion prides, where females do the majority of the hunting.

The rig Mike brings to get off the mountain, believe it or not, is a real thing. It was used during World War II to snatch secret operatives out of Occupied France. Not sure how many died of fright while being saved. A modified version was also used by the CIA and I believe Special Forces during the Vietnam War. Do I recommend trying it? About as much as I recommend trying to catch a dragon.

I'd like to thank my faithful beta readers Janet Guy, Teresa Robeson, Deb deAlteriis, and Donna Fitzpatrick for going through the manuscript with a fine-toothed comb and giving me frank and candid feedback on parts that did not work. All of you reading the finished product owe them a debt of gratitude. And thanks to all the folks at Severed Press who copy edit, create, and distribute Grant's adventures. Special thanks to the amazing cover artists who create works that entice even the most jaded readers to try the first page of my books.

Will Grant end up encountering wooly mammoths? We shall see. Until then, you might want to visit with National Park Service rangers Kathy West and Nathan Toland. They are assigned to Fort Jefferson, a remote park in the Florida Keys. It seems they might be battling giant crabs in the novel *Claws*, out now from Severed Press.

Thanks for reading my stuff. Every page you turn makes my dream come true. Hope to see you at a signing or convention soon. Check my website www.russellrjames.com for my schedule. Say hi at rrj@russellrjames.com anytime.

Russell James
January 2020

Made in the USA
Monee, IL
23 October 2021

80019914R00083